STAR SAVAGE

ALIEN GLADIATOR KINGS, BOOK ONE

Jove Chambers

Punk Rawk Books

STAR SAVAGE

ALIEN GLADIATOR KINGS, BOOK ONE

Jove Chambers

ONE

rowan

"You in the mood for fur, scales, or spikes, sweetheart?" Admii Caspe Tetrone's voice was deep, almost soothing, as he scrolled through the pictures on the holoprojection. He was completely casual about it, as if choosing what flavor of alien man to fuck in front of an arena full of people was just another day at the office for him.

Which, uh, I guess it was.

This was his job. He was a space pirate who dealt in various underground goods, one of which was flesh, especially the flesh of human woman. The Toth liked humans, after all.

There was very little I had going for myself in the universe being a human woman, but there was my sexual desirability, the one thing I could auction off for credits, and now, I was desperate enough to do it.

Caspe gave me a half smile. He wasn't human. He was a ccael, and as such, he had a humanoid upper torso but the bottom half of him was all squirming tentacles. His skin was purple, nearly black, and he was wearing an eye patch over one eye.

That was all.

No clothes.

He didn't have genitalia between his legs to hide. He

didn't have… legs. So, I guessed he didn't need clothing, strictly speaking? I wasn't sure, but I didn't know that his species were warm-blooded, so I guessed the cold didn't really bother him. You wouldn't think a guy like that could be soothing, but he was. He was so blasé about it all that it felt surreal, not shameful, not as though I had hit the very rock *rock* bottom of my entire life.

"You want a recommendation?" said Caspe.

"Uh…" I drew back. "Is that a thing you can do?"

He scrolled past the group of spiky-looking species and the group of scaly-looking species and settled on the hairy ones. "The Treebark people, if this one wins?" He pointed. "Their females don't ovulate unless they have orgasms, so the men have anchor strands which lock on to stimulate females. I hear good things." He shrugged.

I eyed the, uh, man? Treebark person? The one Caspe was talking about. The furry alien was compact, wide, with thick arms and legs and a muscled chest. He had horns that curved around his ears, and fur that grew all over his back. Even though he was obviously not human, even bestial, I couldn't deny he had a certain savage appeal, and I wouldn't say that I didn't like the look of him.

"They make them shave, I think," Caspe said. "For the spectacle, so everyone can see gleaming muscles."

Sure enough, the other species were similarly fur covered with the exception of their chests and arms. It was likely, I guessed. The Toth would like that.

"Might be prickly, I guess," said Caspe, shrugging.

I shook my head at him.

"Not helping?" he said.

"What about the other species?" I cocked my head,

surveying them. They faced forward in the holopics, arms hanging at their sides. I could reach forward and turn each of them around and survey them from all angles. They wore little, only pants or shorts, so their impressive chests were bare. I idly spun one and then another, biting my lip as I looked at the swells and dips of their muscles, their hard stomachs, their powerful arms.

Against all sense, my body started to react to this. Maybe it was the sight of them combined with the knowledge of what I was going to let one of them do to me, that I'd be surrendering to one of these hulking beasts, spreading my legs for him.

I squirmed a little on my chair, feeling tight and warm between my thighs.

Caspe was talking. "Well, if this guy wins, it's nothing special. They're pretty standard, I understand." He shrugged again. He scrolled through, pushing forward another holopic. "And males of his species have coital ties, so that might make it all a little prolonged."

"Coital…?"

"Knots that form in the base of their cocks to lock them in place."

I blinked, trying to think that through.

"Maybe you want to go scaly. I think there's a scarencs in this batch. They have two cocks." He scrolled the holoproj to the group of three scaly aliens.

"What?" I shook my head at him. "What do I want with more than one cock?"

He shrugged again. "So, fur?" He scrolled back.

I eyed the group of furry, hulking, alien male flesh. Apprehension filled me, and then something else rose up on the heels of it, something a little bit naughty, something that might be rightly termed anticipation, even excitement.

Fur.

Beastly, savage specimens. The three of them would fight in the arena. There were three rings, and the aliens were divided according to class today. That wasn't always the case. The Toth might change their fancy at any time and categorize them otherwise. Fur in one ring, scales in the other, spikes in the third. The gladiators in each ring would fight to the death, and I was the prize.

I'd be enjoyed right there on the floor of the arena, thrown to the winner to ravage while the crowd cheered him on.

Caspe was brokering the deal. He'd take a cut, but the rest of the money would be mine. He also assured me that he took my safety very seriously and that I would not be damaged. He couldn't stay in business if he was careless with his girls, he said.

It was horrible.

It was awful.

It was shameful.

I wasn't going to… like it.

Maybe there was some perverse thing that roused in me at the idea of being… I don't know… special? Competed over, desired, and then to have all those eyes on me…

It *was* awful.

But there was a reason I picked this over some other debasing alternative, after all. There were various compensations for this, and it wasn't just the insane payday for a day's work. It did sort of excite me, in a horrible way.

You can back out now, I told myself. I hadn't signed

anything. No contracts were in place. We weren't even at the arena, but planetside. Caspe's ship was docked here and he was brokering deals. He'd take off and take a short trip to the station where the arena was located, and this would all take place this evening.

So, there was still time to call this off.

"Fur," I said, nodding.

"Good choice," said Caspe. "You have a holophoto, or you want to take one?"

"The, um, the nude, right?" I said, leaning forward so that my wrist bracelet was accessible. "Yeah, I got it."

His desk picked up my bracelet and a file folder filled the space, crowding out the pictures of the furry aliens. "Ah, you named it RowanLloxnude, so that's handy."

"I figured you have a lot of girls so if I didn't put my name on it—"

"You'd be surprise how many people don't think of that." He dragged it onto his holodesktop. "And then I've got to rename it, and it's a big pain."

I shrugged. "It seemed logical to me."

"So, we just have some paperwork, and then—"

He was interrupted, as the door to his office slid open vertically.

A human woman walked in. She had deep warm brown skin, and her short dark hair was in tight curls around her head. She wore a similar eyepatch to Caspe. They were called navpatches or something. I didn't know a lot about them, but they helped with hacking into the navigational systems on ships. So, uh, probably a good chance this woman dealt in extralegal jobs, kind of like Caspe. Another pirate.

Caspe was on his feet and across the room way too

fast. I hadn't yet seen him move on those tentacles of his, and it was dizzying.

I swallowed.

He was imposing, especially with a bunch of them stretched out like that, blocking the woman's path. "What do you think you're doing?" His deep voice was cold, not at all rich and soothing like it had been with me. This was a threat.

I hugged myself without thinking about it. The entire atmosphere in the room had changed.

"Looking for you," said the woman, who didn't seem the least bit intimidated by him, even though he was objectively intimidating.

"I'm busy with a client," he said.

The woman gave me a look, through the tentacles. "I'm Admii Sienne Dlach. How you doing?"

"Uh, good." My voice was a squeak.

Caspe rumbled. "Don't talk to her. You know you're not welcome in my ship. You are never welcome—"

Sienne spread her hands. "I need a griplacx coil."

"Well, I need a million credits," he said. "The world's a tough place, and I could give a fuck what you want. Out of my ship."

"I'm stuck planetside, and I thought we could trade."

"No." He gestured with several of his tentacles. "You are my archenemy."

"Don't be dramatic. We compete over jobs occasionally—"

"You poached exactly three lucrative opportunities out from under my nose, one after I had already signed the contract—"

"I do what I have to do, just like we all—"

"Probably because you're a human woman. I bet you

shook your tits—"

"I'll back out of the running for the Gassoricks proposition, how's that? Can we trade?"

"No." His voice got even deeper. "No, I'm trying to conduct business with this lovely lady here, and you are—"

"She's going to do the arena?" Sienne looked at me again. "Are you going to do the arena?"

I bit my bottom lip and didn't answer. I was not getting in the middle of this.

"How much does that pay again?" said Sienne.

Caspe backed away from her. It was like he floated, tentacle limbs askew. "What?"

"You need more girls for that?" She shrugged. "What about me?"

Caspe's mouth opened. His jaw hung open like it had been dislodged.

"How about it?" She grabbed her breasts, and pushed them together. "I'm fuckable, right? I'd do me." She smirked at him.

"No." This was a completely different tone from him. The bottom of his voice had gone out.

"Don't be a gratts, Caspe. Do you need girls or not?"

"You don't want to… do that." He had closed his mouth, but he wasn't looking at her now. "You don't… you know it's in front of an audience?"

"A Toth audience," she said.

"There are cameras."

"I need to get off this planet. It's important. I can handle it. How bad could it be?"

"Bad," he breathed. And then he seemed to remember me, and he cringed. "Uh, sweetheart, do you think you might wait outside the office until I conclude this business with my, um, colleague?"

I stood up. "Why is it bad?"

"You'll be fine." He said this very quickly.

"I'll be fine too," Sienne said.

Caspe turned back to her, and I suddenly realized something. Caspe was *into* her. Like, they had a whole complicated, competitive sexual tension thing going on. He was trying to talk her out of it because he didn't want some other man fucking her.

Of course, Caspe *couldn't* fuck her?

I didn't know a lot about his species. Maybe he had a retractable cock in with all those tentacles?

"Sweetheart." Now Caspe sounded irritated at me. "Outside."

I couldn't help but smile. "Yeah, sure, okay." I pointed at Sienne. "I already picked fur. Don't think you can poach that from me."

She raised her eyebrows. "Fine. Not much into hairy chests."

"They make them shave their chests," I said.

Caspe glared at me.

I left the room.

The door snapped shut after me.

I leaned against the wall in the narrow outer corridor of his ship. I waited.

Several hidosecs later, the door opened.

Sienne stepped out. "I don't see why you don't just take the holophoto yourself."

"Yeah, *I* don't want to see your tits," he growled at her. "Use the camera on the entertainment deck." He pointed at an open door.

She shrugged at him. "You're going to see them anyway, right?"

He turned back to me, ignoring her. "You ready to sign the paperwork, sweetheart?"

"Sure," I said.

Grouchily, he brought up various documents on the holoprojection.

I scrolled through them moving my finger through the projection in front of me. "You know, you could just trade her for the coil thing."

"Did anyone ask you your opinion?"

"That would stop her from doing the arena, you know. And anyone can see you don't want her to do it."

"Shut your pretty mouth, sweetheart," he said in a rumbling voice.

I shrugged. I signed one of the documents and kept scrolling.

"Oh, you need to initial there." He pointed.

I initialed.

"I don't care what she does," he told me. "I hate her."

"Yeah, it's obvious how much you hate her." I smirked.

"What's that supposed to mean?"

I shook my head, grinning. Not only was he into her, he was in denial about it. Adorable.

"Uh..." He put his hand in the middle of the projection, breaking up the image so that I couldn't read it. "Look, what I said about it being bad?"

I straightened, all humor leaving me.

"It's usually fine," he said. "But occasionally, there are, uh... certain species... let's just say the Toth don't care much about casualties, considering these are fights to the death, after all. They like blood, and they like sex, and they like the two of them together. There's nothing dangerous-looking in the fur set, I don't think, though. You should be fine. If there was something, and that gladiator happened to win, or if anything looked hinky, I would pull you and run. You'd forfeit the credits, but you'd be alive, you know? That's my guarantee. I promise you. I'm not… I mean, I'm a scoundrel with no moral compass, but pretty dead girls really harsh my mood, so…" He pulled his hand back through the projection. "Anyway, just, I swear to you, okay? I wouldn't let anything happen."

I swallowed hard.

"You have one more place for your signature," he murmured.

I hesitated.

"I promise," he repeated.

Still, I hesitated.

He scrolled up and pointed at the part of the contract that stipulated the compensation. He circled the number with his forefinger, disrupting the projection, making the string of numbers seem to float in the air. "I figure you need the credits, am I right, sweetheart?"

I signed.

* * *

hugo

They distributed the discs with the girl's holopic and I almost didn't bother looking at it, because I didn't even want to think about that part.

I'd never done a fight like this, not one of the big ones in this arena. My handler wanted it, and I refused, and we went round and round. He got paid big money to put his gladiator's life on the line, after all. Huge money in compensation in case I didn't make it out.

Of course, it didn't matter to him.

The Toth were not a particularly empathetic species, even with all that human blood mixed in. It was their culture, too, I supposed. Back before my life was a series of bloody physical gauntlets, I did have time to contemplate things like that—whether people were born cruel? I figured the Toth *could* change. But why would they?

What possible inducement did they have to change their ways? They were the top of the food chain, and they subjugated all of us to prove themselves, to celebrate their triumph, and because they were all supremely assured of their superiority.

Anyway, my handler…

My *owner*, if we wanted to be blunt about it.

He knew that a gladiator had to get himself into the ring under his own steam, or the fights didn't happen. There were various ways to motivate a man to put his life in danger, to even give up his life, and they mostly had to do with the people that man cared about.

There was a reason I'd agreed to be a gladiator after all.

But he hadn't found that thing yet. He hadn't found a way to threaten my family, considering the current stipulations of my contract, and so I wouldn't do these fights.

Finally, he put the only thing in front of me that would motivate me.

Freedom.

If I won this fight and I fucked the girl and entertained the cursed crowd, then I went home, and my stint as a gladiator was over.

I hadn't fucked a girl in…

Well, how many gecycles had I been under this contract?

And before that, once I'd failed to have a mating reaction to any of the women in my entire clan, that had put an end to any more attempts, so, it had been a while.

I'd never been with a human, not even back in the days before I'd been locked into this, when my family had sent me off to the university, and I'd seen other species in the classrooms and on the streets of the capital city. Before the Toth toppled the last vestiges of any semblance of galactic regulation, before everything was despair.

I knew about human women, though.

They were popular, if only because of the Toth preference for them. Soft, small, mostly hairless, with a muted array of skin tones. They were widely compatible with a number of species in terms of mating, versatile in that way.

Finally, I looked at the disc.

The girl I'd have to fuck when I won, and I had to win.

I wasn't looking forward to killing two other gladiators today, and it wouldn't sit easy on my conscience, because I knew they were likely rulers in their own right, brought here because of the same reason I was, to save their people, to keep the Toth from harming those they were responsible for.

But there were clauses in the contracts for death in the arena, and if they died, they'd die secure in the knowledge they'd protected their people.

That is, as long as the Toth followed the contracts.

If they didn't, we had no recourse. We were under their boots and we had no way to fight back.

It might be my hands and my might that killed the other gladiators, but it was the Toth who would be responsible for their deaths. None of us had a choice, and we all knew it.

I didn't entertain the possibility that I was going to

die.

My first fight—not one to the death, but even so, all fights are dangerous, and accidents happen—a seasoned grizzled gladiator gave me a piece of advice. He said that thinking about outcomes gave them power in your mind, and that it was best to let there be no negative power before a fight.

Much of a fight was chance. Only a little of it was skill.

Since the odds were stacked against a fighter, he should use every shred of advantage he might have at his disposal. Thinking positive probably only made a negligible difference, but it might be the increment I needed to prevail.

Maybe I looked at the disc and thought about fucking the girl because the situation was so surreal and so ugly that I couldn't—even still—descend into it enough that I could really believe it was real. To think this was what I was, that my life and the lives of men like me were routinely offered up for entertainment, that we were worth so little.

The full emotional rush of the implications of that truth?

Unbearable.

I didn't think it. Never thought it, not if I could help it. It was despair. Everything was despair, and despair was untenable.

So.

Fucking. The disc. The girl and her breasts and hips and thighs, all of which she had in ample supply. She seemed as small and soft as the human women were advertised as being. Her skin was pale, paler on her breasts and belly. Her nipples were rosy, pert against her skin.

I looked at the disc and I felt aroused and I felt ashamed of myself.

This was all another layer of discomfort for me.

They wanted to make us beasts, but we weren't.

They wanted us animals, violent and rutting, and the fucking, I knew that it wasn't supposed to be, uh, gentle and sweet.

The girls were volunteers.

Well, I didn't know if anyone in the entire galaxy besides the Toth were capable of true voluntary actions anymore. We were all coerced in various ways.

What sort of situation did a woman have to be in that she agreed to being violently taken in front of an audience by a strange man who had just killed two other men?

It certainly wasn't the sort of thing a woman would enjoy, I didn't expect.

So, *sure*, volunteers.

They also received some kind of monetary compensation.

She knows what she's getting into, I told myself, gazing at her picture, turning her holo around to see her from all angles.

But why would she do this? She looked so breakable, so fragile and small and easily bruised. Maybe it was just the lack of hair. Maybe it was because women of my people were usually larger than human women.

I shook my head and tasted metal in my mouth.

Could I do this without hurting her?

I had to at least try.

There was the fact I couldn't speak Common, though, so we likely wouldn't even be able to communicate. I could understand it. I could even write it. But due to a brutal fever when I was young, I'd suffered an injury to my vocal cords, and many of the noises that Common required—most of them taken from the dominant Toth tongue—were impossible for me to articulate.

When I was a chieftain—rich and educated—I had a mechanical device I could wear that would speak for me, but that wasn't deemed necessary for a gladiator.

It meant that I had difficulty communicating with other fighters, but this didn't really bother me. Isolation was better. I could speak a few other languages, including my own native tongue which wasn't spoken outside of the planet Abbunia, so I got by. Being mute except for a lot of growls had its advantages anyway. If I intimidated others, that was an advantage I could leverage.

My existence was all about survival, not about things being pleasant.

This girl…

Why did she seem like the only pleasant thing I'd been offered in cycles and cycles? Why did I want that suddenly, with a fierce desire that was almost painful?

I switched off the disc.

No point in looking at her any longer.

No point in thinking about it.

I had to fulfill my contract, and I knew it. If I didn't fuck the girl, I didn't get my freedom. It was part of the performance, and it was what the audience wanted. My handler would look for any reason to weasel out of our agreement. I had to do exactly what I was contracted to do.

So, I would.

TWO

rowan

"Oh, one of the scaly ones has two dicks, apparently," I said.

The third girl who'd be the final prize was named Elodee Wilth. She'd arrived just after I'd finished signing my contract, and I'd been off getting showered and coiffed for my performance tonight. I was nervous, but I was pretending like I wasn't, which was why I was making offhand comments to Elodee. We were sitting in a lounge on the ship, both in robes, both smelling of lavender soap and cosmetics.

Elodee had olive skin and long, dark hair. She gave me a look. "Caspe thinks two dicks is a selling point. He told you too?"

I shrugged.

"Well, what are the odds that twin-dick lizardman wins?" She grimaced.

"You worried about it?" I said.

"No, I'm serene and utterly unaffected by the enormity of what I've signed myself over to." She was sarcastic.

I smirked. I liked her. "Yeah, I get that."

"I'm not doing it for fun, you know."

"Hey, you don't have to feel ashamed of yourself," I said, pointing to my own chest. "I also signed up for this."

"Well, I don't have a choice," she said.

"Neither do I," I said. As previously indicated, that wasn't entirely true. There was always the option of going to the factory planets, but people worked literally to death there, and it would take me years to make what I was going to make in one day, doing this. I also could have gone for straight-up prostitution. There was always a market for human girls, even if it was just so some guy could feel like a Toth hii grax with his dick in a human. But that would have taken longer too, because it wouldn't have paid nearly as well.

She sighed, rubbing a hand over her face. "Caspe give you the spiel about how he'll keep us from dying?"

I tensed and didn't answer.

"I can't see how that makes sense for him. The Toth would be pissed at him for backing out on a contract. He'd ruin his entire business. What's one stupid, desperate girl against all that?"

"This is reassuring." It was my turn to be sarcastic.

"Sorry." She stretched her neck. "I think I'm just trying to distract myself from the two cocks."

"Yeah, death is totally preferable to that," I said.

She grinned, looking away. "Totally." She laughed.

"I think we're both probably just..." I shook my head. "This is so surreal."

"Right?" She shivered. "Where's the other woman?"

"You haven't met her?"

"I saw her coming out after taking her nudes," said Elodee. "She seemed completely unfazed by everything. She was wearing that navpatch?"

"Yeah, she's a pirate like Caspe. She seemed... really tough and capable and, uh, cool."

"Very cool," said Elodee, nodding.

"Oh, my ears are burning."

Elodee and I both stood up.

Sienne sauntered into the room in her own robe. "I'm not a pirate."

"Right, I'm sure you have a term you prefer, like, uh, personal property reliever?"

Sienne snorted. "I mean, I don't steal things."

Elodee and I must not have looked convinced.

"I scavenge," she said. "Seriously. And if my whole ship wasn't made entirely of haphazard junk, I wouldn't be in this position." She sat down heavily on a chair and bowed her head, rubbing her forehead. "There's other things. I don't have a choice either." There it was, in her voice too, the same desperation that I had felt every morning when I woke up for the past gemoon, ever since my father died, ever since the guys he owned money to decided I'd have to pay his debts.

A gemoon was the length of a moon cycle on the planet Geheri, the homeworld of the Toth. Most of our standardized measurement of time came from the Toth. Gemoons took approximately thirty-two gesuns—that is, the time it took from sunrise to sunset on Geheri.

"Do you, um, you want to talk about it?" said Elodee in a soft voice.

Sienne lifted her gaze to Elodee's. "*You* want to talk?"

Elodee shook her head. "Not particularly."

"Me either," said Sienne. "And about Caspe? You're not wrong. He'd say anything for a payday, and he doesn't care about anyone except himself. Do not expect him to come to your rescue."

I hunched up my shoulders. "Nothing's going to go wrong. Women do this all the time, and they're fine."

"Let's talk about after," said Elodee. "After, when we have the money, when we can fix things."

"Right," said Sienne, sitting up straighter. "That's what we should definitely be focusing on. I can handle a rough lay, trust me. Might even be a little fun." She gave us both a wicked grin. "Am I right?"

I flushed, but I was smiling too.

"A little adventure," said Sienne, sucking in a deep breath.

"Right." Elodee's voice was a little bit throaty.

"Hey," said Sienne. "After this is over, you need a safe ride out of this system? I'd be happy to help you out."

"That's nice of you," said Elodee, a note of wariness in her voice.

"I figure this whole situation is all about treating us like animals," she said. "Entertainment. Nothing. The least we can do is be humane to each other, yeah?"

"Yeah," I said, strength creeping into my voice. "Well, after it's done, I don't have a ship or anything, but once I've transferred some credits, if there's anything I can do for either of you… let me know."

"Ditto for me too," said Elodee, giving us a smile.

"We're going to be fine," said Sienne, also smiling.

"Right," I said.

We all nodded at each other. It might be bravado that the three of us were projecting, but maybe bravado was exactly what we needed.

THREE

rowan

Once docked at the space station where the arena was located, there were slews of people everywhere, and we were moved through the place like we were on an assembly line. Caspe lounged in various spots, observing, following us from room to room.

We were still in the robes he'd given us, and everyone who attended us was incredibly respectful, Miss Llox this and Miss Llox that, asking if there was anything they could get us and actually following through on our requests.

We waited in a vast room with thick, comfortable chairs, long walls of mirrors, and tables of fruit and sweet delicacies.

Unfortunately, I wasn't much in the mood for eating.

There was a sparkling alcoholic beverage on ice, though, and a few small bottles of sickly sweet berry liqueurs that were made on planets on the Nevis system. We all drank.

I didn't want to be so drunk that I was stumbling or anything. Just enough to take the sharp edges off everything.

After a time, we could hear the distant roar of the crowd, and we were all led out of the room and taken to the wings outside our respective rings. At this point,

I lost track of Caspe. I would have put money on his having followed Sienne, though. Or maybe not. Maybe he wouldn't want to see that, and he'd stuck with Elodee.

I was surrounded by a group of Qel attendants, all female. None of their heads came much higher than my shoulders, and they all spoke quite quickly, in accented Common. They informed me that I'd have to go out into the middle of the arena for everyone to see, including the gladiators.

Of course I had to do this nude.

I had known this, but even as the moment approached, I clutched my robe. I didn't know why I cared, but it was somehow my dignity that I was going to voluntarily take leave of, and I wasn't sure how I felt about that.

The attendants chirped at me, telling me that if I didn't remove the robe myself, they would have to take it off me by force, that the audience always liked that.

I threw it off on my own, squaring my shoulders, and I walked out into the arena.

The ring was raised, floating on thrusters in the air. It and the other rings could move, and they rotated from high to low and top to bottom, so that people in all areas of the arena could see them. Of course, the fights were filmed, and there were large screens overhead, each projecting one of the rings, and people also brought it up on the holoscreens on their bracelets.

The hisec I stepped into the ring, I also appeared on one of those huge screens and likely on the small screens of most of the audience as well.

But I didn't really pay attention to that, because now, I was closer to the aliens who were going to be fighting over me. They were in archways, chained at the wrists and the ankles, and at the shouted suggestion of the crowd, they surged forward, straining against their restraints, to get to me.

My heart leaped into my throat and began to thump loudly at my neck and my temples.

I eyed the sharp fangs that protruded over the lip of one of the men, and then the size of one of the other's meaty, huge hands, which looked as though he could crush my skull with one palm.

And then my gaze settled on the Treebark alien, the Abbunian. He was growling and straining at his chains like the others. These guys were all under contracts, and they had to put on a good show or there were consequences.

I knew how this worked.

Some rich, careless Toth noble took his father's ship joyriding and landed on one of the technologically underdeveloped planets. Then, he blew something up with the weaponry that the Toth all had. For sport, they said. Hunting is a manly pursuit and what-have-you, and besides, those aliens are all savages. And everything not a Toth is an alien. Then this rich gratts demanded to see their leader, and he offered a trade. Sign yourself over to me as a gladiator or I destroy your people.

They always signed themselves over.

So, I knew these gladiators didn't have any choice, and that there were likely threatened consequences if they didn't play to the crowd.

It had been made clear to me that if I felt frightened, I should go with it. Screaming was encouraged.

I didn't scream, though.

The Abbunian looked lethal like the rest of them, but there was something in his eyes, something almost sad.

I let my gaze travel over his body, and he was looking me over too. They were all looking at me. They were only strides away from my naked flesh.

His muscles contracted and rolled under his skin. His shoulders were massive. His forearms were huge. He wore only a pair of black shorts that clung to him and left very little to the imagination. He was well endowed. He was the one with the anchor strands?

What did that even mean?

Our gazes suddenly met and locked.

His lips parted, and the look he gave me was part apology and part heated hunger. He wanted me.

My mouth was dry. I wanted him back.

What if he didn't win?

I looked at the other two aliens, just as muscled, just as lethal and bestial.

Neither of them met my gaze.

But then I was being dragged back out of the arena, back to my attendants, who praised me as they put the robe over my shoulders and took me to the seat where I would watch the fight.

I was suddenly very invested.

I leaned forward, gripping the railing in front of me, as the arena erupted in cheers and all of the gladiators were released.

Sometimes fights involved weapons, but not always. It apparently lasted longer when they had to kill each other with their bare hands, and the Toth liked the fights prolonged, because of course they did.

The ring with the furs swung away from me, spinning through the air, to settle down low on the other side of the arena.

Now, the ring in front of me was the spiky gladiators, all of which looked pretty horrifying up close. I winced for Sienne, even as I searched the screens for the one depicting the fur fight. I hadn't been allowed to wear my bracelet into the ring. It was probably for the best. I wouldn't want it damaged. But I couldn't bring up a holoscreen on my own. I had to watch the screens.

Of course, maybe it wouldn't get damaged. I wasn't sure if the Abbunian one wouldn't be a little careful with me. He seemed…

Oh, this wasn't good. Of all the things to happen to me, to get some weird attachment to this gladiator? Maybe it was some kind of survival instinct, my body trying to bond somehow to lessen the brutality of what would happen to me?

But where was he?

The furs were circling each other, taking each other's measure. If the gladiators took too long to engage, the rings would shrink, forcing them closer, so I imagined that wouldn't go on for too long.

Sure enough, my Abbunian made the first move. He launched himself at Fang-man, head down, running directly into the other man like he intended to run him down.

Fang-man absorbed the impact, however, and they grappled.

I clenched my hands into fists. Fang-man was bigger than my guy, and I didn't want anything to happen to him. I was nervous.

Fang-man might win, Rowan, I told myself. *Fang-man might fuck you.*

I burrowed into my robe. This was appalling, that's what this was. Why had I signed myself up for this?

My Abbunian abruptly tipped Fang-man over his shoulder, causing Fang-man to land face first and roll out of the fall. Agile for a huge thing, he rolled into a crouch and was upright but obviously dazed.

When my Abbunian rushed him from behind, Fang-man toppled forward.

My Abbunian kicked him while he was down.

Shrieks of approval from the arena.

He kicked him again, a blow to the back of the skull.

But the other gladiator, Big Hands, engaged my Abbunian, punching him from the side.

The Abbunian turned his attention entirely to Big Hands while Fang-man struggled back to his feet.

Big Hands was good with his fists, and my guy was bleeding in minutes. Blood was gushing over his face, over his mouth and lips and down over his chest.

I hugged myself in some feeling I couldn't quite identify. I hated seeing him hurt. I hated that this was even happening, that this was a fact of the universe we lived in. It was all horrible.

And yet there was something affecting about the way they all looked together — grappling, gleaming, and sculpted, something that my body was responding to in... I don't know... something primal, perhaps? Something deep in the recesses of the beginnings of humanity.

Sometimes the Toth made ridiculous claims — that their ancestors had gone through the wormhole and "made" humans, set things up to make my species evolve, just so they could come back generations later and abduct females.

I didn't believe it. Here was a galaxy full of species that seemed to have evolved just fine without any outside help, and the fact that we were all so similar, it pointed not to Toth involvement, but to something innate in the way life *worked*.

When life emerged, it followed a set pattern, and the reason for that was *not* the Toth.

Maybe I just didn't want to believe I'd evolved precisely for the purpose of being an alien fucktoy.

Of course, stars, look where I was now.

Anyway, I hadn't grown up on Earth. I was third-generation Colony, and I hadn't known my grandparents, who *had* been abducted. I didn't know a lot about humanity, but I understood that we were not unique in our process of advancement. Humans had some technological advancement—more than the Treebark people of Abbunia but less than the Toth—but we all, Toth included, started out as primitive as the furry creatures I was watching fighting in front of me now.

And I couldn't help but feel as if this entire display was powerful precisely because it rang that same bell within all of us, Toth and alien alike. We had ancient knowledge of this—fight—mate—fight *for* a mate. It resonated within us all, and this was why the Toth set up these games. They were entirely disconnected from that primeval aspect of themselves, and the only way they could even touch it was through this spectacle. It was why they were rabid for it; why they couldn't get enough.

As I was thinking this through, the rings moved again, and the ring with the furs spun and swung so that it dangled in the air just below me, close enough that I could lean over and see, but just far enough that I couldn't have possibly leaped down into it.

I did lean over.

The gladiators had all frozen in place while the ring moved, clinging to the floor or the sides. It wasn't unheard of for fighters to go over the edge and fall to their deaths. The Toth considered this a feature—not a bug—to the floating ring design.

Now, the gladiators were upright, and the fight began again.

There was a roar from the crowd and it jarred me, but I realized they were reacting to something that was happening in one of the other rings. I almost looked up at the screens, but I didn't want to take my eye off my Abbunian either.

It wasn't looking good for him.

Big Hands and Fang-man had decided to gang up on him. Fang-man was behind him, arms wrapped around my Abbunian's biceps, holding him in place. My Abbunian's chest gleamed with sweat and blood. He was breathing hard, and I watched his chest rise and fall, the swells of him undulating with his movement. He was beautiful.

I clutched the railing harder as Big Hands punched him.

I screamed as the blows came down on him. I couldn't help it. I wanted him. I didn't want to watch him die.

You're going to see death, Rowan, I snapped at myself. *Two of them are going to die.*

I knew this. And it wasn't as if I hadn't seen these sorts of fights before. I'd never been a guest at an arena, of course, but they were broadcast all over, on screens in pubs and in people's homes. They were sport—a source of betting. How do you think my father got in so much debt, anyway?

It was different, though, on a screen, than right here, so close.

My Abbunian heard me, and he looked up.

Our gazes met again.

My expression must have been full of terror and anxiety, and his had been grim frustration. But when he locked eyes with me, he smiled at me.

My breath caught in my throat.

My Abbunian slammed his head back into Fang-man's face.

Fang-man staggered backwards, howling.

My Abbunian was free, and his smile widened. He glanced up at me again, and he looked downright cocky.

My heart skipped a beat.

He tackled Big Hands, and they were a whirl of limbs and fur, their two bodies moving against each other on the floor. He slammed his fists into Big Hands. He used his elbows and his legs, and he pinned the other gladiator to the floor. His back was entirely covered in fur, but I could see his powerful muscles rippling under it, and he was perfection. He moved exactly like a man should move. My heart was still beating out of rhythm, and now I didn't know why — was it fear or arousal and what was *wrong* with me?

My Abbunian got up, his posture sure, bouncing on the balls of his feet.

Big Hands stayed down.

My gladiator looked up at me, with an expression that seemed to say, *What do you think of that?*

I cheered. I applauded.

There was blood running down the hard planes of his stomach muscles, and I didn't know if it was his or one of the other gladiator's, but it did horrifying things to my insides.

My body was starting to feel too warm. I pulled my robe tighter against me, sure this wouldn't help my temperature, but I was ashamed of myself for my reaction. This was the wrong reaction.

Fang-man rushed my Abbunian.

He stepped out of the way and Fang-man collided with the other side of the ring.

My Abbunian hurled himself after him.

They grappled at the edge, Fang-man tipped backwards, his mouth wide open, his throat exposed as he scrabbled at my gladiator's midsection.

And behind them, Big Hands was slowly and painfully getting to his feet.

Finish him, I thought, hating myself for it. *Throw him over the side.*

But then the rings moved again, their ring spinning as it headed for the other side of the arena.

Fang-man went over, jerked by the sudden movement.

But he yanked on my Abbunian, pulling him with him.

My Abbunian tipped over the side.

Fang-man lost his grip, screaming as he tumbled down, down, down.

My Abbunian's feet came up off the floor of the ring.

I shrieked.

But then the ring stopped moving, and he righted himself, feet back on the floor.

And now, the ring was all the way on the other side of the arena, and I couldn't see anything. The scaly gladiators were in front of me now, and I looked up for a screen to find my ring again. What was going on? Was he all right?

I located a screen.

My Abbunian was sitting on the inside of the ring, back against the wall, clearly shaken.

Big Hands was staggering toward him. Big Hands's

face was a mess. His cheekbone looked as if it had been broken, judging from the sunken shape of half of his face. He was swollen and bleeding and hulking, some kind of monster dragging himself across the ring.

And my Abbunian wasn't even on his feet. He was too far away for us to exchange looks.

My entire body was alight. I was on edge. It was like electricity was running through my limbs.

My Abbunian pushed himself up to his feet. He gritted his teeth, clenching his fists, and launched himself at Big Hands.

More fists flew. More grappling, as they grasped at each other, yanking each other's fur. Once Big Hands got hold of one of my Abunnian's horns and hurled him all the way across the ring.

But neither of them went down and stayed down.

It went on and on. It felt interminable to me.

Sometimes Big Hands had my gladiator pinned down, and sometimes my gladiator was on top.

Sometimes they were both on their feet, trading blows and shaking off droplets of sweat and blood.

The rings moved again, but they didn't come back close to me.

I could see they were both exhausted. They were wounded and bleeding. They were sweaty with exertion.

Then Big Hands somehow got his foot onto my gladiator's hand and he slammed his heel down over and over.

My Abbunian rolled over, cradling his wrist against his chest, his face a mask of pain. I could see from the way it dangled that his hand was broken.

Big Hands pressed his advantage, aiming a kick at my gladiator's chin while he was still in a crouch.

My Abbunian's head jerked back, droplets of sweat flying through the air.

Big Hands went for another kick.

My Abbunian caught his leg in the air before he could make impact. He favored his good hand, but he used the broken one too, and he tugged hard.

Big Hands's other foot went out from beneath him. He landed on the floor of the arena, the back of his skull bouncing slightly against the floor. He was stunned. He wasn't moving.

My Abbunian stood up, standing over him. He wiped at his mouth with his good hand, wiped away blood and sweat as he surveyed the motionless gladiator.

Had he done it?

Was Big Hands dead?

My Abbunian grimaced and rolled his shoulders. He brought his own heel down on Big Hand's face. Once. Twice. Three times. Big Hands's face caved in, nothing but bone shards and blood and meat.

I looked away, the sight of it too much for me.

Suddenly, there was music and lights and the rings were swinging around, and the announcer was coming over the loudspeaker to announce one match over, a winner victorious.

My attendants were back, urging me to my feet.

I stood up, shaky with adrenaline and nerves.

He'd won.

My Abbunian had won.

I was relieved, but then I realized I didn't know why. He... the image of Big Hands's ruined face swam in my memory even as I tried to shove it away. I had wanted the Abbunian. I still wanted him. But I was afraid of his brutality and his strength and his viciousness. What was he going to do to me?

Dazed and apprehensive, I didn't make any resistance as the attendants herded me back to the archway where I'd gone out before.

They pulled the robe away from my body, and I didn't fight them when they did that either.

Then we waited as the ring docked with the archway.

Before, the attendants had chattered constantly, but now they were quiet. Perhaps they realized there was nothing to say to me in this moment.

I had an awful thought that I was not going to be able to do it, that my legs would turn to jelly and refuse to support me.

But no, that wouldn't matter. I'd seen women try to escape before, and they always overpowered them and threw them to the winners anyway, and the crowd always loved that.

My teeth started to slam noisily against each other.

Maybe I was cold?

Was it cold?

I looked down at my arms and realized that there was a fine pebble of bumps there, but was that from cold or just… just…

The ring docked and men in uniforms rushed past me into the ring to drag out Big Hands's body. I hadn't even noticed they were here waiting. They had all seen me naked.

I had to laugh at myself.

Everyone had seen me naked. I had gone out into the middle of that ring and *everyone* had seen.

Then Big Hands's body came back through, and the laughter choked me, because he was so much worse up close.

I might have whimpered or something. I don't know. One of the attendants put a reassuring hand on my arm.

I shook her off.

I didn't want to be touched.

That made me want to laugh again, except it came out sounding more like a sob. I was going to be very much touched. That was happening.

Someone spoke to me, telling me I needed to go out. That if I didn't, I'd be forcibly put into the ring.

I drew in a shaky breath and I walked forward. I had the oddest sensation, sort of that I was disconnected from my feet. I was bobbing along as they moved, but I couldn't feel them properly. The archway jarred up and down in front of me as I walked and then I went through it and into the ring.

The ring smelled like blood and sweat.

My Abbunian — *was* he mine, though?

The Abbunian was standing in the middle of the ring, head down, holding his broken hand to his chest.

I got closer.

He looked up. His gaze settled on my breasts.

I stopped moving. My breath came out loud. It seemed to echo off the sides of the ring. I didn't know why I could hear it. The arena was nothing but noise — the crowd cheering, the other fights — but here, I felt insulated from all of it.

His gaze slid up to my face. He licked his lips. His face was streaked in blood. It was smeared this way and that from where he'd rubbed it. He tried a smile, but it was tentative. The apology from before, it was in his eyes.

I should have kept walking, should have closed the distance between us, but I couldn't move. My teeth took that moment to chatter again, and I clenched my jaw to stop it.

He winced and looked away.

I kept my gaze on him. Up close, he was even more beautiful than I'd thought. I had grown more attracted to him over the course of the fight, and he was... positively perfect, a work of art, the male form at its pinnacle. I dragged my gaze slowly over his bare shoulders and chest, over his thighs, every muscled part of him. He was gleaming with sweat—bloody, wounded.

My body clenched, somewhere deep inside. I was frightened of him, but something in there was waking up again.

Still, I didn't move.

He did.

He took several steps forward, closing the distance between us, and he said something to me, but it wasn't in Common. It was some harsh guttural language with throaty, growly consonants.

I jerked back at the sound of it. Didn't he speak Common?

He reached out with his good hand and caressed my shoulder and said something else. The tone sounded apologetic, or maybe that was in his expression.

I understood, though. I nodded at him. I touched his shoulder, reassuring, permissive. We had to do this, and I knew it.

For a moment, we froze, hands on each other, and then the crowd, who was watching us, began jeering over us. I couldn't make out the words, but I knew they weren't here to watch us touch each other's shoulders and they didn't want this gentle.

He said the same thing he'd said before in his

language, the apology-sounding thing, and then his hand urged down my shoulder, over my shoulder blades, and planted firmly, fingers splayed, against the small of my back.

His hand was *huge*. From the span of his thumb to his smallest finger—they had four fingers—he took up my entire back.

My heartbeat sped up. My chest rose with my breath.

He pressed my body against his.

His skin was practically scalding hot, but then he'd been exerting a lot of effort. The sweat got on my skin. The blood got on my skin. And I smelled *his* sweat, the slight difference of it from the general sweaty smell, his own distinctive scent, which was… dizzyingly good.

I relaxed into him, hands going up to his shoulders.

His pelvis jerked against mine. His cock was hard inside those little black shorts he was wearing, and I felt that, and it was good too.

I tilted back my head, gasping, exposing my throat, and he leaned in to taste it.

His hand went lower, still holding me against him, but now cupping my backside. He pressed his hardness into me, and I wriggled against him. I could feel heat pooling between my thighs, and I was turned on by this.

I was freaked out and ashamed and confused too, but there was arousal here.

His tongue on my clavicle, flat and dark—almost brown—as he lapped at me.

Odd, but arousing, too. It felt good.

It dipped down, between my breasts.

I gasped, tilting back, allowing him to hold me up, but giving him access.

The crowd cheered, and I was reminded they were there, that they wanted to see me, wanted to watch, that I was experiencing this intensity but that it was because of them that I had to feel it.

His tongue licked one of my breasts, a long thick lap from the underside, over my nipple, and up to the top, and it felt very good, and I didn't care—not for that instant—that the crowd was there. His tongue was a little bit textured, though soft, and the sensation was heady.

I ground into his pelvis.

He rewarded me by licking my other breast.

I moaned, wriggling into him. He could do that all day as far as I was concerned. My nipples agreed. They were hard little eager nubs. They weren't the least bit confused. They were shameless and greedy.

He squeezed my backside and held me against his erection and licked me again and again and again.

FOUR

I'd heard other gladiators claim that fighting made them horny, but I personally didn't get that. A fight made me want food and a shower, maybe not in that order, and then sleep. I was exhausted after a fight, and the thought of more exertion, it sounded ludicrous.

Added to that, I was currently in a great deal of pain. I was pretty sure that there were several bones in my hand that were broken—maybe shattered—and I was covered in cuts and bruises.

But, roots and branches, when she walked into the ring…

I had never gotten so hard so fast. She looked amazing. I'd been attracted to her before—the picture in the disc, and when she'd been brought out and shown to us in the middle of the ring. I'd seen the way she looked at the other men and the way she looked at me. More than that—I'd scented her, and she'd smelled turned on. Afraid too, maybe, but the arousal scent was there.

And then, she'd been cheering for me.

She chose me.

I had known I had to win, but there had been moments, moments where I was losing my will to continue, where the idea of giving over to death and failure felt like a warm blanket of softness—an end to my constant existence of pain and violence. I would have thought the prospect of freedom would have been enough, but it was *her*. Her gaze, locked onto mine, her expressive brown eyes, that was what had pulled me through.

And then she was there, in the ring, nude, beautiful, and mine.

I scented her again, and this time, the fear scent was stronger, but my cock didn't care. I was ashamed of myself, but when she trembled, it made me harder. I wasn't—I *couldn't*—be turned on by her fear. I wasn't that sort of man, was I?

But it didn't matter.

I had to take her, whether she was afraid or not, and I couldn't even talk to her. I tried, but she obviously didn't speak my language, and why should she? It wasn't even one of the official languages of the planet of Abbunia. It was just our clan's language, spoken amongst my people.

I tried to say, "I'm sorry." I tried to say, "You're beautiful."

It didn't matter.

My cock was throbbing. My need was threading through my body with a power that rivaled anything I'd felt in the ring, and I put my hands on her, and I was gratified that my touch triggered her arousal scent.

I tasted her, and she was smooth and soft—there was something to be said for human women, wasn't there? I buried my face between her soft, wondrous breasts, and then I tasted them too, and this we both liked.

If I weren't in an arena, if it wasn't this, what I would have liked to do was lay her out somewhere, limbs splayed for me, so that I could look and smell and taste her everywhere, especially between her thighs, where her scent was concentrated. It was a sweet, tangy musk, and it was intoxicating.

I could have probably licked her for hours.

She would never have complained either, I could tell that. She might have been frightened before, a little soft, shaking bundle of a thing, but in my arms, I had brought out her pleasure and surrender, and I could tell from the half-lidded look of her eyes that she was mine.

Mine.

A sudden surge in my cock.

I let go of her, I was so surprised by it.

No, no, no, not now, I thought, frantic.

She lost her balance. She slipped on a small puddle of blood on the arena floor and went down sprawling, limbs askew. She cringed up at me.

But I was struggling to keep control of myself, because this was happening, at the most inopportune time. I'd felt it before, maybe a time or two, never this strong, and never for a female who wasn't of my species.

The sensation of the mating madness was traveling up my spine, and I grunted, rolling my shoulders, my back, fighting against it. I had shoved it down before. It was possible. It was just... it was stupid... it was probably because I was so turned on. My body was confused by the intensity of it, and it had sent this out instinctively, at the worst possible moment.

She was still on the floor. She was looking up at me, confused, concerned.

Her fear scent was coming back, coming off her in waves.

Maybe that would calm my mating instinct? I

breathed in it.

Nope. My cock was turned on by it, stupid cock, stupid…

Curse my cock. Curse my mating instinct.

Curse everything.

I felt it hit the back of my skull, like a burst of sparks in my brain. I threw back my head, panting, overtaken.

I was lost.

* * *

rowan

I scrambled backwards, an awkward crab walk, knees bent, hands behind me.

I didn't know what had happened to the Abbunian, but he had dropped me, and now he was writhing in front of me, head thrown back, making a very threatening sound in the back of his throat, and I was freaked out.

If this was part of normal sex for these guys, this was a thing that Caspe could have told me about. What was going on?

I collided with the side of the ring.

The Abbunian toppled forward on his hands and knees. He bared his teeth, his gaze fixed on me. He was like an uncaged beast, a freaking animal. I flattened myself against the side of the ring, breath coming in gasps.

My body was so freaking confused right now, swinging back between being afraid and being turned on. My nipples were still tight and tingling. It was warm and slick between my thighs.

He came for me, scrambling at me too fast.

I shut my eyes, putting up my hands to ward him off.

Distantly, I could hear the crowd roaring. They were

probably loving this.

When I opened my eyes, he was on top of me. He rubbed his face against mine, rumbling in his throat, licking me again, but this time, I felt the scrape of his teeth. I whimpered.

He'd done away with those shorts of his at some point. Maybe when my eyes were closed?

Okay, whoa.

There he was.

He was definitely well-endowed. He was as thick as my wrist, and the head of him was that same dark nearly-brown color, like his tongue. It was glistening, likely with some pre-ejaculate and it was, you know, kind of beautiful.

There were the anchor strands. They were writhing, like little prehensile hairs. They surrounded his package, wriggling strands that encircled his very hard cock and his scrotum. It was dark too, and I had an odd thought that I should just reach out and cup him there and that would probably tame him.

He touched me first.

He pushed my thighs apart, settling himself between them, and he dug his fingers into my skin.

I yelped.

He winced also, but this was because he'd used both of his hands, as if he'd forgotten that one of them was broken because he was so intent on fucking me. Since he only had one hand, he had to let go of me to grab hold of his cock, holding it between his thumb and thick first finger. He positioned himself—completely in the wrong spot—and pressed the head of himself against me. It slid into the right spot because I was far more turned on than I had any right to be.

I screamed.

He was huge.

He was big.

He was stretching—

Oh.

What was that?

The *strands.*

They had burrowed into me, all around me. One was plunged into my skin just above my clit. But they hadn't… penetrated my flesh like a needle. They weren't exactly… they were like little strands of energy, like electrical pulses, and they, um, they *vibrated.*

I screamed again, but it was a *different* scream.

The vibrations went through me all around me, little electrical ripples of pleasure, and my entire sex convulsed in a shudder of sweetness.

He adjusted us, fingers of his good hand against my hip, getting himself in position to thrust. When he pulled out, the strands stretched, tugging on my sensitive flesh.

Fuck.

The sensation of the strands, of their tug and vibration, coupled with the fullness of his fat cock crammed into me? I was falling apart. It was good. It was *too* good. I was…

Fuckfuckfuckfuck—

My hands were clutching him—his shoulders, his arms—lower—his backside.

"Yeah, *there,*" I told him. "Deeper."

He pumped his hips against me, I held onto his perfect butt and urged him on.

He braced one arm against the wall next to me. He panted, his gaze finding mine.

Ohhh…

I kissed him. I put my mouth on his and tangled our

tongues, and his textured tongue was like fireworks all through my body.

I cried out, breaking the kiss.

He kept his mouth on me. He started licking me again.

I couldn't *take* that.

His tongue found one of my nipples again.

Starbursts. In my clit. Inside my cunt. Behind my eyes. Bright and hot and gushing and intense.

And then again. Better and more intense this time, and then—

Oh, not *another* one…

It was the *mother* of all orgasms.

I went limp against him, tears in my eyes, my entire body twitching as he slammed himself home and jerked his own climax into me. I could feel him inside me, like my own orgasm turning inside out, like our climaxes were mingling and I couldn't tell where mine ended and his began, and…

Fuck.

I'd never had an orgasm during intercourse before.

I collapsed into the wall, dazed, out of breath, destroyed.

He draped himself over me, letting out rasping breaths. He was talking again, in that language, way too many words coming out of his mouth, but I didn't care.

I kissed him again. I pulled back and stroked his blood-streaked face, and I couldn't even say what I felt for him at that moment. It was bigger than an exploding sun. "Good, Abbunian," I said. "I'm glad you won. I'm glad it was you."

He searched my gaze, giving me a tiny smile, as if he'd understood me.

I laughed. "You are… fantastic." I stretched out all the syllables in fantastic. "You're really great." I laughed again, a throaty, pleased laugh. Yup, would have to tell Caspe that he had been right. Those strands? Good things, indeed.

He shook his head, extricating himself from me, and the lack of his cock was a disappointing sensation.

I let out a little noise at its loss, reaching for him.

He caught my hand with his and spoke urgently to me. Then he shook his head, muttering something that must have been a swear word or something. I could tell from the inflection.

I sat up straighter, curious now. "What?" I said. "What is it?"

He gestured back and forth between us. He looked up, as if thinking. His shoulders sagged.

Suddenly, the ring moved.

I cried out, launching myself at him.

He tightened his arms around me, reassuringly rubbing my back.

When we settled, the ring was swarming with people. They helped him to his feet and gave him a robe, and my attendants were there with a fresh robe for me. They led me away.

The Abbunian shook off his guards and tried to come after me, but they stopped him, lifting tase sticks that sparked threateningly.

Right, right.

I was a one-time prize. He didn't get me again. But he was trying to tell me something, and I wanted to know what it was. Also, I was feeling very stupid, very female responses to amazing sex. I'd never had sex like that, and I tended to get a little gushy and mushy over the normal kind. I hadn't fallen for him or anything, but I had a tender fondness for him, and I found him even sexier than I had before, and I didn't necessarily want us to be separated either.

I might have tried to get to him.

My attendants yanked firmly on my arms, scolding me.

Reluctantly, I let them pull me out of the ring, away from him. But I kept looking over my shoulder at him, where he was, behind the guards, gazing at me with a feral intensity.

The attendants tugged, chirping their disgust and disapproval.

"What's his name?" I said. They had names. Maybe no one bothered to call them anything in the ring, not typically. Sometimes, if a gladiator was really good and had a long, lucky streak of a run, he'd get enough notoriety to have some moniker placed on him. My Abbunian wasn't that way, though. "There's got to be a record of his name."

The attendant shrugged at me.

I could see the judgment in her eyes. What had it looked like to her? That I'd been brutalized there and liked it, and now I was lovesick over the beast who'd fucked me into submission?

I tried to feel ashamed of myself, but it had been a really good orgasm and shame was a hard feeling to find right then.

Anyway, it was pointless.

He was a gladiator. He was under a contract. I could never fuck him again, not unless I started to follow him around and volunteered to be the prize for every one of his fights.

My mouth went dry at the prospect.

No.

I wouldn't…

No.

I squared my shoulders. Best to forget about him. I was lucky that it had been so pleasurable for me. It could have been a lot worse. I should be pleased at my good fortune and leave it at that.

I had credits to collect after all.

FIVE

hugo

Roots and branches, I'd mated to her.

It shouldn't even be possible for me to do that, right? We were not the same species. I'd never heard of another Treebark person mating to a human. Of course, I wasn't sure if anyone else of my species had ever had sex with a human either.

The mating bond wasn't complete.

She hadn't accepted it, which was the final step that needed to be accomplished before we'd be bound entirely. But I was one-sidedly bound to her, anyway. My strands had locked in on her, transferred information about her to me, and I'd become attuned to her body. I would now only become aroused for her, not for any other female.

I knew that occasionally a female rejected a mating bond, and the man's bond eventually did wear off, but that was a very rare thing. So rare that I had no idea how long it would take.

I had wanted to tell her.

But...

Well, it didn't matter. This was some freakish, stupid thing that had happened to me with her, and she wouldn't want it. She wouldn't agree to the mating bond with me in any case. It was only that the things she'd said to me afterward, it was kind of obvious it had been good for her and that she didn't, well, hate me.

Which… well, I supposed we only had the mating bond to thank for that, because if the strands hadn't locked in on her, they might not have known how to pleasure her so thoroughly. Even my own strokes had been informed by the information I'd gotten through the strands. I knew when she wanted it harder or slower or deeper.

Well, she'd been a little vocal with the instructions too, which had been…

Roots and branches, that had been the best sex of my life.

Obviously.

Bonded sex was like that, or so I'd heard. I'd never bonded. People didn't always, anyway. Sometimes people got older and no mate had presented itself so they just paired up with someone they felt mostly compatible with, even if the biology didn't agree enough to connect them.

Since I'd never bonded to any of the women in my clan, I'd assumed that would be me too. It was a process, the bonding. The mating instinct rose from scent supposedly. It rose for a potential mate. Then the strands connected, and they either locked in or didn't.

I still didn't understand how they could have locked in for her.

Hugo, this woman sold her body for rough sex with a gladiator in front of an entire arena and to be possibly replayed by anyone who had the vid copy. You don't want that sort of woman for a mate.

I pushed back on that. She was probably desperate. She probably didn't have a choice. She was afraid of me. She didn't seem the sort to have done it as a cheap thrill.

Roots and branches, *was* there really a sort of person who did something that demeaning and dangerous as a cheap thrill?

I supposed it wasn't out of the realm of possibility, but I knew my own circumstances were complicated and coerced. It was likely hers were as well.

However, I did need to remind myself that the mating bond was a physical thing. It meant that we were well matched biologically to have biologically favorable offspring, and it didn't have a thing to do with how well we'd be matched personality wise.

I liked her, though.

I didn't know her.

I didn't know a thing about her, and I liked her.

"...paying any attention to me," came a voice.

I blinked. My handler was there. How long had my handler been here? "I'm sorry," I said. I wasn't speaking my clan's language with him, but rather Cobran, a trading language based on a combination of the languages of the Lanisson sector. My handler was conversational in it.

"You all right?" My handler pursed his green lips. The Toth looked a lot like humans in many ways. They were shaped similarly, and they even had five fingers and five toes. They were also similarly hairless, even more hairless than the humans, who had tufts of it on their heads and in various other places. The Toth were smooth all over. But they had a lot of variety in skin tone, unlike the humans, who were fairly muted. Toth mated with humans a lot, but the skin genes seemed to be dominant and drowned out the humans' tans and browns, even in half-breeds.

There were Toth women again, thanks to the humans and a few other compatible species. Of course, nearly all Toth were half-breeds now, not that this bothered them, since they all believed their superior genetic material wiped out the others'.

My handler though?

He was not naturally hairless. He had to shave.

Noticing his stubble always pleased me for some stupid reason. I just liked seeing the proof that they were not genetically insurmountable, I supposed.

"Of course you're not all right," said my handler. "Your hand."

"Oh," I said dumbly. I lifted my arm and surveyed the way my hand dangled. Now that I was thinking about it, that did hurt. However, the pain was such a constant throb that I'd started to become accustomed to it.

My handler grabbed it, his five fingers running over the back of my hand and my wrist, exploring.

I grunted at the pain of that.

"I'll be right back," said my handler, letting go of me.

Grimacing, I cradled it against my chest again.

When my handler returned, he brought one of the med workers with him. The worker had a bot with long, spindly appendages, and it set to work seizing my hand none too gently.

I grunted again, but the bot immediately injected me with some kind of local anesthetic.

Ah, the relief of that. I sagged, letting out a noisy breath.

My handler snapped his fingers in front of my face. "Okay, then? You can focus?"

"Fine."

My handler glared pointedly at the med worker,

who was looking at the readings on the bot's screen and not paying us any attention anyway, but whatever.

"Fine, *my barith*," I said sourly. My handler was the Loth Nongg, loth being a title of Toth nobility, and he insisted on proper address whenever anyone could hear. When the two of us were alone, he seemed to acknowledge that I hated him, obviously, but in front of others, I needed to pretend to respect him.

He gave me a smug smile. "I want to talk about renegotiating your contract."

My lips parted. I was stunned and hurt, but why should I trust anything that came out of his mouth? "You made me a promise. I signed documents." I'd read them eighteen roots-deep times, looking for loopholes. But I wasn't trained in the Toth law, so there might be something that I hadn't noticed, I suppose. "I won. I'm supposed to be free."

"No, I realize, and you are." He glared at me. "After all the revisions we had to go through before you signed that thing, of course there's no way I can legally keep you now, but I thought maybe we could talk about your staying on."

"Never." Agonizing pain shot through my hand, even through the anesthesia. I cried out, trying to jerk my hand away from the bot, not that I could.

My handler turned to the med worker. "What are you doing?"

"Almost done," said the med worker.

"This, for instance?" said the handler. "I'm paying for this." He nodded. "I don't have to do that. Our business relationship is concluded."

"There's the ship you owe me," I muttered.

He rolled his eyes. "Obviously, there's that. But why take a ship when you and I could make a small fortune together? I'm willing to make you a very attractive offer. I'll give you thirty percent of any of the money I make on your fights, both in the compensation from the gladiator league and in any bets I win."

I snorted. "No."

"Half. Fifty percent," he said. "I never saw you fight like that before."

"Because I wanted to be free," I said. Even though maybe it was that girl.

His shoulders sagged. "What about… a fight-by-fight basis? I could serve as your agent." There were gladiators who did this, who'd made their way out of their contracts with handlers and went into the business on their own, taking the profits for themselves. "I'd take the standard cut, twenty-five percent. You'd get the bulk of it."

I shook my head.

The bot released my hand. It was numb, but when I flexed the fingers in front of my face, it seemed entirely mended. That was what Toth technology could do. I knew what he'd just paid for—bone mending— wouldn't have been cheap.

"But Hugo, for the sake of all the stars in space, can't you see what we could do together?"

"I just want to go home," I said. "But thank you for fixing my hand."

He folded his arms over his chest. "You could send every credit home to your clan. Think what the money could do for your people."

I hesitated. Sometimes, gladiators negotiated contracts that meant lots of money was funneled back to their homeworlds, but I had given up a lot of that so that I could get clauses in that would protect every member of my family and my clan. I didn't want their safety ever used against me. So, I wasn't going home to riches, but at least I'd never been forced to make terrible decisions. I thought it was the right call, but I had to admit that I was drawn to the possibility of what my handler was offering me now.

I could do one more fight, take the profits, and run.

I was quiet, thinking.

I meant to ask if he'd insist it be another fight to the death. Instead, I said, "What's her name?"

"Whose name?"

"The prize. The girl. She has to have a name, right? There's got to be some way to find her?"

He let out a disbelieving laugh. "You'd think you'd never fucked a human."

I shrugged.

"Oh, really?" His mouth curved into a smile.

"Never mind." I squared my shoulders. "I need a shower."

"What if you think about it?" said my handler. "What if you take a shower and mull it over? Sign up for another fight and let me be your agent, and I'll find that girl's name for you. Stars in space, Hugo, I'll hire her for you for a couple gesuns."

I winced, shaking my head. No, he made it sound like she was a prostitute, that her body was just for sale.

She could be, spoke up a voice in my head. *She could be a professional, and maybe that's why —*

I was mated to her. It didn't matter.

Your body is mated to her. It's a biological, involuntary thing that happened, probably because you haven't gotten your dick wet in far too long. It doesn't mean anything.

"Mull it over," said my handler again, still smiling that awful smile of his.

Curse that man.

rowan

I was able to get my bracelet back now that the fight was over, but I didn't have any clothes here on the station. They were back on Caspe's ship.

I snapped my bracelet on and checked to see that the credits I'd been promised had been deposited in my account. They were there, but oddly, Caspe's fees hadn't been taken out, which didn't make any sense.

I checked the screens in the corridors, but they were all showing the fight between the scaly gladiators. The spiky fight was done then? I guessed that Sienne was done getting used by the winner too, because if that was happening, that would be on some of the screens.

I hurried to the dock where Caspe's ship was.

The dock was empty.

Red lights were flashing and lights were beeping, indicating the ship had left the dock without permission and probably owed the docking fees that had to be paid before leaving. Someone like Caspe, though, probably knew how to hack the codes to get out of that. Pirates did.

He was gone.

He had taken my clothes and abandoned me here. I went back to the arena and to find Elodee and tell her the news.

But the scaly fight had just ended, so she was going to be busy. As luck would have it, the guy with two dicks had won after all.

I could have stayed to watch, but I didn't. I just pulled up my contact list on my bracelet and started scrolling through it, looking for someone who I could call who had a transport that could go from planetside to the space station to pick me up and who was still speaking to me.

The list was surprisingly short.

When I ended up being hunted by all the groups my father owed money to, it was odd how quickly all my friends stopped responding to my messages.

It really only boiled down to one person, and that was Nich.

Nich was like a big brother to me. I'd been close to his actual younger sister Jeffi, who had been killed when we were teenagers, a freak joyriding speeder accident, tragic and abrupt, the worst thing that had happened to me before being on the hook for all my dad's incurred debts.

Nich and I had gotten pretty close in the wake of it. We both needed someone to talk to about Jeffi, and he had latched onto me because I was sort of a younger sister surrogate for him. Whenever he had the urge to do something big brotherly, I was the one he called. Similarly, when I needed someone, he was always there for me.

This of course meant that I had a huge crush on him, one that I drunkenly admitted to him only about two gecycles ago, and he had shut me down hardcore, because he saw me like a sister, obviously. It was obscene to him to think of me as a sexual being.

He had broken my heart, and I had steered clear of him for the most part since. Messaging Nich was an exercise in mortification and pain, and it was going to be twenty times worse if he'd seen the fight tonight.

But, well, I had known this would happen if I did the arena, and I'd chosen to do it anyway.

My phone projected a list of contacts in the air and I hovered there, highlighting his name with my finger, hesitating.

I wondered what the Abbunian had wanted to tell me.

I wondered where he was. Could I go and find him somewhere in the station?

No, that was a bad idea, I figured. I doubted they let human girls into the rooms where the gladiators were kept. I bet that wouldn't be a really safe proposition for me.

With the way my guy had rushed me there at the end, completely savage and out of control, well... would he do that to me again?

My pussy clenched at the prospect, eager.

Darkly, I addressed her. *Down, girl.*

Definitely not great to let *her* make decisions. She did not have my best interests at heart. She just wanted another orgasm.

I punched Nich's name. A screen popped up, and I dictated out a quick message. *Hey, you busy?*

A query popped back, video request from Nich.

Well, then. I accepted it, and a holovid of his head projected up out of my bracelet.

"You're okay," he said, looking me over. "You're okay, right?"

"Oh, you saw it," I muttered.

His eyes widened. "Why didn't you... You know that if you needed — "

"I needed credits, Nich, more credits than you have, or could ever get your hands on, not that I would have let you give me them even if you'd offered. Anyway, I'm only calling because I need a ride? I had one lined up, but I got left behind. Do you feel like coming up to the space station?"

"Oh, yeah, I could do that." He nodded fiercely. "Yeah, definitely. See you soon. What dock?"

"Uh..." I didn't know that. The public dock was a bad idea, considering everything. There had to be a special dock for my comings and goings, but I needed to check on that. "I'll find out and send you a message, yeah?"

"Sure. I'm going out the door now. I'll be there as fast as I can."

"Thanks, Nich."

"Least I can do," he said. "Be safe until I get there, Rowan."

"I'm fine, Nich," I said, a little annoyed, but also warmed by his obvious concern for me, considering there was no one else who felt that way, no one at all.

SIX

hugo

A shower cleared my head well enough to know I would never step into the ring again, not unless I had no choice. It wasn't worth it, even a fight that wasn't to the death. Accidents happened all the time.

Roots and branches, I'd almost gone over the ring earlier that night. Falling to my death was not the way I wanted to go out.

I knew my mother and sister, and what they would want more than anything was me home safe and sound, not all the credits in the galaxy.

I sought my handler out, and he wasn't pleased.

We went round and round. I insisted he tell me where my ship was docked, since that was a stipulation of the end of my contract. I was supposed to be given a ship so that I could get home.

He wanted to give me a first class ticket back to Abbunia.

I should have known he hadn't set this up. He never intended to let me go. I told him that a first-class ticket to Abbunia was worth less than a ship, and that it wouldn't help me, because I would dock in one of the cities and have no transport home.

He had no ship, though, so then we haggled credits. He said he could just give me enough money to buy a ship.

Sure, fine.

I had never bought a ship in my life. My father had bought me the one I had back in my university days, and he'd bought it on Abbunia, which was a far more backward planet than the planet closest to us, Kalion.

So, I didn't know the first thing about how many credits I would need or what to look for in a ship. I was going to get screwed in this deal, and I knew it.

Alternately, he offered that he would get me a ship within the next few Kalion sun-cycles, less than five, he claimed.

Five suns?

No, I wanted to leave now. I wanted all this behind me.

So, I negotiated him up on the amount of credits he wanted to give me, and he caved too easily. I negotiated higher, until he started showing some resistance, and even then, I couldn't tell if he was faking it.

Roots and branches, I hated that man.

But I walked away from the encounter with a bracelet and credits—hopefully enough credits for a ship.

I had to take public transport planetside, and everyone was astonished to see me there. They started to ask for autographs and pictures, but when I responded not in Common but in the growls of my own language, they backed off and gave me a wide berth.

I went scrolling through stats on the feeds, looking for the girl's name. Nothing. Should have known the Toth wouldn't care about noting those sorts of things. They didn't even bother with most of the gladiators' names. We were all body fodder.

But then I remembered that I had access to the schedules and rosters for the fights in the arena, and that listed names for fighters, so maybe it would have the prize's names.

Sure enough, there it was.

Rowan Llox. It listed her home planet too, and that was Kalion, where I was heading.

I started making a few queries in the public records. Taxes and the like were all accessible if you knew where to look, and I might be able to find an address.

I did. Actually, I found about three. She seemed to move around a lot from year to year. I saved them all to my bracelet. I hadn't committed to the idea of going looking for her or anything. I didn't really know why it was that I was expending so much effort looking for her.

Seeking her addresses took all of the length of time waiting for the transport, the entire ride to the planet, and then some time after we'd docked. I stayed in the spaceport, sitting on a bench, scrolling through documents on my bracelet, looking for addresses for her.

When I was finished and I couldn't find anymore information, I told myself that I'd go look for a ship, not her.

But it was late here in this city on this planet, the middle of the night.

Nothing was open.

I certainly wasn't going to be able to buy a ship at this hour.

Conversely, I didn't much imagine she'd be pleased to have me show up at her door either. I didn't know if she'd even gotten home. Maybe she was still on the space station. There was no reason to go looking for her, anyway. I was sure she wouldn't want to be mated to me, wouldn't even care about the knowledge of that.

It was only…

Well, shouldn't she have the choice? If we were really this biologically compatible, and if she'd liked me as much as she seemed to have, wouldn't she want to know? Hiding the fact I was mated to her, never giving her the option, that didn't seem right to me.

* * *

rowan

Nich seemed embarrassed on the ride back from the space station, especially considering I was only wearing a robe. He didn't seem to know where to look. He couldn't meet my eye, but he couldn't look at any other part of me either, so he spent a bunch of time pointedly not looking at me, even though the ride back and forth between the planet and the station didn't involve a lot from him. Mostly it was all about locking into the tractor beam from either station. The distance was quite close. The arena orbited Kalion.

I was too embarrassed to talk either. I didn't like thinking of Nich seeing me like that, seeing that happen to me. It was an exercise in mortification, that was for sure, and I inwardly cursed Caspe for leaving me. And why hadn't his credits been taken out of my payment? Was he persona non grata at the arena now? Why? Because he hadn't paid his docking fee?

I expected Nich to drop me at home and leave, since everything was so awkward, but instead, he invited himself in and went rummaging around for alcohol.

I went to shower quickly and change into clothes and when I came back, he had poured us shots.

"You need this." He shoved it at me across the

65

counter that served as my table and the only surface I had available for food prep. This apartment didn't so much have a kitchen as it had a wall. The counter pulled out or it could be shoved in and a stove and sink could be expanded instead. It was all very compact, but that didn't mean I didn't pay more than I could afford for it.

Currently, I couldn't afford much of anything. I'd had to leave my job when the debt collectors got in there and got my entire paycheck diverted to them, leaving me nothing. What was the point of continuing to work if I couldn't eat or pay rent?

Nich took his shot, grimacing a little at the strong taste.

I surveyed mine. "I'm really fine. It wasn't that bad, overall."

Nich raised his eyebrows. "Wasn't that bad?"

I shrugged. "Didn't I look like I was having a good time?"

"You were screaming." He blinked at me. He poured himself another shot. "Oh," he said in a different voice.

I flushed. "We don't have to do this," I whispered. "We don't ever have to talk about this."

"So, that's what gets you going, huh?" His voice had a different quality to it, now, almost playful. He downed the shot, letting out a wry chuckle.

"No," I said. I shrugged. "I mean… I'm just glad it wasn't horrible, you know? If I had to do something that demeaning, the least I could get out of it was an orgasm."

He looked up at me, shaking his head. He was smiling.

What was that smile? I drew back.

He nodded at my full glass. "Take the shot, Rowan."

His voice was lower in pitch than usual.

My lips parted. Oh, the way he was looking at me, it was… I took the shot.

"That actually makes me feel better, weirdly." He ran his finger around the rim of his shot glass.

I went around him, opening the small cool box that I had stuffed full of non-perishables. "I need a chaser." I seized some carbonated sweet beverage and drank it straight out of the bottle. But now we were close, standing next to each other, not on either side of the counter. I stopped, looking up at him from beneath my eyelashes, holding the drink bottle between us. "Nich, what's going on with you?" I whispered.

"I just never saw you in that way before." He was whispering too.

I swallowed.

"You, uh, you…" His gaze flicked down over my body and then back up to my face. "You're really all right?"

I nodded. "I'm fine."

"It would still be, uh, be really messed up of me to take this moment to make a move, wouldn't it?" He searched my gaze.

I opened my mouth, and no sound came out.

"Don't answer that." He turned away, pouring himself another shot. "You don't have to think about that. That's way too much for you after the day you've had."

"Well… what sort of move?"

He looked at me, grinning again, the boyish grin of his that always made my heart stutter, and this time was no exception. I'd wanted Nich for cycles and cycles. He was my first real crush, but I had filed him away as nothing more than a friend a long time ago.

For this to be happening, really happening, after all this time? He rubbed the back of his neck. "Uh… seriously? I'm supposed to find some smooth way to answer that?"

I stepped closer to him, tucking a strand of my hair behind my ear. "We talking like kissing or… or full-on hooking up?"

"Kissing," he said in a very deep voice. "Obviously, after everything, you wouldn't be…" He shook his head. "Wow, I can't believe that you did that, Rowan."

"Me either," I said.

"You would think it would…" He lifted his hand and let it hover next to my face. Then, slowly, softly, his fingertips made contact with my cheek. "That it would turn me off, knowing some other man had been with you just hours ago, but… I don't know… it's, uh, it's…"

I pressed in closer. Now our bodies were practically touching. "It's what?"

He lowered his face, lining us up. He was going to kiss me.

I shut my eyes.

He kissed the tip of my nose.

I opened my eyes in protest. "What was that?"

He kissed my forehead. "Rowan, you're *you*."

"What does that mean?"

"It means that if we're going to do this, I want to do it right, and I don't think right is jumping into something when we're both a little tipsy and after you've been through all that. The last thing I ever want to do is hurt you. If it's going to happen, we should take our time."

That was actually sweet. I gave him a little smile. I should have known that if Nich was going to be with a woman, he'd be like this, honorable and careful.

He was still touching my face. His fingers traced the outline of my jaw. "So, uh, I'm going to go home."

"Don't," I said. "I'm actually… I'm kind of hungry? You feel like picking up something from the all-night diner and chowing down with me? We could just hang out."

He considered. "I did just have three shots, so if you're going to want me to be super in control of myself, you should probably kick me out."

"No," I said. "I trust you. You're Nich."

He brushed his fingers over my chin. "Yeah, but Rowan, you are… I just didn't realize how incredibly sexy you are."

I shivered, liking that. I put my hand on his chest. "Well, if you get really out of control, I can probably handle it."

He raised his eyebrows, letting out an affected breath. "I saw that you could handle out of control, yeah."

I flushed again.

"Sorry," he said. His voice was a little husky.

I bit down on my bottom lip.

"I'll get food," he said. "It's just around the block, so I'll be back soon. You sit tight."

"I can put the order in on my bracelet," I said.

"Sounds good." His fingers lingered on my face. He kissed my forehead again. "Okay, see you soon." He pulled away and went around me, past the counter and through the small lounge room to the front door.

Once he was gone, I busied myself tapping in various things on the menu, ordering lots of greasy diner food.

When I was done, I poured myself another shot.

What were the odds?

So, this thing I'd done, it had felt really good, it had gotten me enough credits to get out of debt, and now Nich was interested in me. This was the first good day I'd had in a very long time. Maybe my streak of bad luck was ending.

The entry query on my door beeped.

Nich already?

He knew the code.

Who else could it be at this time of the night?

I went to the door and palmed the controls, allowing the two sides of the door to slide open at eye level.

Fuck.

My Abbunian was standing outside my door.

SEVEN

hugo

It was her.

First address I tried and I lucked into finding her.

"What are you doing here?" she said.

I started to answer but then I remembered I couldn't speak Common. I fumbled with my bracelet. I could type in Common, and if I brought up a screen, we could communicate that way.

She opened the door the rest of the way. "Come in, of course. You don't have to stand out in the corridor." She looked me over, her breath coming in little gasps.

I stepped inside, unable to take my gaze from her. I'd forgotten how pretty she was. Her features seemed perfect to me now, the ideal of femininity, and I liked how my presence seemed to affect her. She didn't smell afraid at all. In fact, I could detect a hint of an arousal scent coming from her.

My cock responded immediately, half-hardening in the pants I was wearing. It was interesting to be dressed around her.

She was smiling, looking me over. "You're, um, I thought you'd be at the arena. Don't you have a contract? Why are you here?"

Right, I needed to get my bracelet working.

"Oh, you can't speak Common," she said. "How *did*

you find me?"

I gestured to my bracelet.

She nodded. "Yes, that's a bracelet. Do you have access to my address somehow? Did they give you that just because we, you know, fucked? Oh, what am I doing, you can't even understand me."

I shook my head furiously.

"You *can* understand me?" She narrowed her eyes.

I nodded.

"So, then why can't you speak?"

I gestured to the bracelet again, bringing up a keyboard, and I started to type, but she stepped closer, then, and I was hit with another wave of her scent. My balls tightened and I went from half hard to rigid immediately.

And then…

Roots and branches, my mating instinct was rising again. It was twice as intense as last time, twice as quick as well.

I struggled against it, and I knew it was happening too fast, that I was going to lose.

It burst at the top of my spine, and everything changed.

My body went into an instinctive mode, and I was barely in control of myself. I rushed her.

She shrieked, fear scent coming off her in waves.

We went backwards into a cushioned bench she had against the wall.

I tried to apologize, but she couldn't understand me, and it was difficult to get the words out. I tried to stop myself, but I couldn't do that either. I seized handfuls of the shirt she was wearing and ripped it open, ripped open the supporter she was wearing over her breasts as well.

She put her hands on my shoulders and pushed.

I tried to fight it. I gritted my teeth and tried to stop.

But the madness was strong, and my instinct had taken me over. I was powerless until I buried my cock in her wet heat.

* * *

rowan

I was plastered into pillows in my living room, my clothes shredded, and my Abbunian was licking me.

I had been struggling until the licking started.

Now…

Oh, I meant to struggle. I *should* struggle. This was so fucked up. This was not the way things were done. Maybe on his backwoods planet, a guy could just come into a girl's house and tear off her clothes and start going at her like it was nothing, but this was not the way things worked in civilization, and this was crossing a line.

It was only that his textured tongue made it hard for me to think, and he was currently lapping at my breasts, lingering to swirl around my hard nipples, and it felt so good. Every lick was a dart of goodness that tunneled down into my core, and my pelvis tightened and heated in anticipation of what was to come.

His hand was healed now, I noted. He was using both of them to unfasten his fly and take out his cock, which was just as big and pretty as it was the last time I saw it. I wondered what it would be like to suck it.

Why was I thinking about further debasing myself for this man who was forcing himself on me?

Traitor, I shouted inwardly at my body.

My eager little pointed nipples did not mind being traitors at all. In fact, I was pressing my chest up to his mouth, arching my back, helping him get at my breasts.

73

He dug his fingers into my hips again and yanked me into place, not the least bit gentle, and then his humongous cock was pushing its way into me.

I cried out.

I was sore. He was big, and I had apparently not taken that as easily as I had thought. I could swear it hadn't hurt before, well, except maybe right at the beginning before his strands—

Ah, sweet relief as the strands attached. They pushed electrical pulses into my muscles, relaxing them, easing the way I gripped him, and I could also feel wetness rushing into me—was that me, or him? Did his body make wetness on command if I wasn't wet enough?

But I couldn't think about this, because the strands were doing their little vibrating thing, and everything felt amazing.

I had once seen this diagram of the human female clitoris, how internally there was a whole lot more of it, and it extended all around the vulva under the skin. The Abbunian's little strands pulsed into me in all those places. One was even sending tiny electric jolts into my taint, and it was all…

Good.

I moaned, pumping my hips against the huge, thick cock that had invaded me.

I was nothing but a gushing, squishy, wondrous thing of bright lights and pleasure. I was gasping and groaning and clinging to him, and every movement he made felt twice as good as the last one.

He was licking me.

Then kissing me, tangling up our tongues.

Then licking me again.

Then flicking my nipples with his tongue.

Everything was good. Candy sweetness and fluffy

clouds. I was soaring somewhere near the horizon. I was shooting right out into space and bouncing off the stars.

Tremors went through my pelvis, promises of things to come.

The tip of him seemed to swell, and he moved himself, angling himself in a very clever way. What was that spot, and why didn't I know it was there?

I cried out, a sharp cry of delight.

He said something to me in his growly language.

"Yeah, it's good, baby," I told him, touching his face, stroking the hair that grew long on the back of his neck. "It's real good. Don't stop, okay?"

He replied something growly and reassuring.

"I didn't think you would," I muttered. "Not that this is cool, by the way, because you totally didn't ask permission."

I was almost ninety percent sure he said the thing he said to me before, and that it was *I'm sorry* in his language.

"Don't be sorry, ask!" I snapped. Then I threw my head back as my pleasure expanded and went bright pink and intense. "Oh, whoa," I managed. None of the other noises I made were remotely intelligible, nor were they really words.

I felt as though I was tugged out of my own reality and deposited here, in an ever-expanding sky of bright colors and tufts of softness and explosions, one after the other, blooming in clusters as I came again and again and again and—

The door opened.

My eyes snapped open, and I locked my gaze with Nich over the Abunnian's shoulder.

He dropped the bags of food, and diner grease

splattered all over my floor.

I was still having orgasm aftershocks.

The Abbunnian was in the middle of coming.

Nich got out his bracelet and started punching in emergency services.

"No!" I tried to shriek, but it came out garbled. I scrabbled at the Abbunian's chest, trying to push him off, although why I was trying when I hadn't been able to budge him before, I didn't know.

I concentrated on getting words out, stopping Nich, but instead, I was distracted by the fact that the Abbunian's upper pectorals were smooth, and that he did *not* shave his chest. Well… my hands went lower. Maybe here, on the underside, there was some stubble. I glanced away from Nich and at the Abbunian's chest, imagining it with dark hairy accents around his muscles, wanting to see what it would look like. I made a little noise in the back of my throat.

"Emergency services, how can we serve you?" chirped a voice from Nich's bracelet.

I slammed my palm into the Abbunian's chest and shoved.

He went backward, but I thought he pulled himself away.

"Nich, hang up!" I said, scrambling to my feet. "You know I'm on the debtor list. They'll lock me up if they come here."

Nich furrowed his brow at me. "You have credits."

"Yes, but a transfer of that size is locked down for two business suns before I can make a withdrawal, you fucking idiot."

He slapped a hand over his bracelet, cringing.

I stood up, throwing up my hands.

"I'm sorry." Nich came across the room and picked

up a throw blanket and wrapped it around me, covering me. "You were being… assaulted and—"

"I'm fine," I snapped. I glared down at the Abbunian. "I mean, I don't know where you think you have the right—"

He was typing furiously on a holoscreen projecting from his bracelet. He hadn't even bothered to fasten his fly. *I mated to you. I have a mating instinct and I can't control it. I'm sorry.*

I drew back.

"What?" said Nich. "What in stars' sake is that? And what is he even doing here? What happened?"

"I mean…" I shrugged. "He stalked in here and ripped off my clothes and started…"

"Assaulting you," said Nich, glaring at the Abbunian.

"Well…" I furrowed my brow. "I mean, is it still assault if it feels good?"

"Yes," said Nich, nostrils flaring.

"Feels really good, like impossibly good, like out-of-this-world—"

"I get it," said Nich tersely.

Fuck. I eyed him. That… whatever was starting between us? It was done. I was pretty sure it was done. And it hadn't even had a chance to start.

I looked down at my feet, snuggling into the blanket he'd wrapped around me.

This was a mistake, typed the Abbunian. *My apologies. You won't hear from me again.* He got up and put his clothes back in order as he went for the door.

"Wait," I said.

The Abbunian turned. He brought up his bracelet and typed again. *Your boyfriend's right. Doing that to you was wrong. I wouldn't have done it if I was in my right mind.*

He's not my boyfriend. Instead, I said, "I don't even know your name."

Chieftain Hugo Benetriel of the Treebark people of Abbunia. Again, my sincere apologies. He palmed the door controls and the two sides slid open horizontally. He stepped out and the door snapped shut behind him.

He was gone.

I gazed into his wake.

"They would have clocked the address that I called ES from," said Nich.

I turned to him. "Oh, stars, you're right."

"And it'll pull up my info and address since I used my bracelet, so we can't go to my place," he said.

"We?" I said hopefully. "You still want to be around me?"

"I'm not going to blame you for something that was obviously against your will," he said. "What kind of guy do you think I am?"

"Oh," I said softly.

"Your credits from tonight? After you pay off everything you owe, will you have anything left?"

"A little."

"Enough to pay me back if I get us a room somewhere tonight?"

I nodded fiercely. "Yes, definitely, yes. Thank you, Nich, thank you so much."

"Yeah, not a big deal." He shrugged. He was doing that thing where he wasn't looking at me again, though.

I parted the blanket to reach out and put a hand on his shoulder. "Nich, I know you—"

"If we're going to get out of here before the police show up, you better get dressed."

"Right."
I pulled my hand back.
Right.

EIGHT

rowan

Nich got a room with double beds, and he turned off the lights right away and climbed into bed.

I tried to talk to him a couple of times, and he said that he was exhausted and that he wouldn't be any good at keeping up a conversation right now.

I got it.

He was conflicted. He might say that it didn't matter that he'd walked in on me with the Abbunian — with Hugo. I lay on my back and tried the name out. I liked it, and when I thought about him, I got a sort of fluttery, happy feeling in my stomach.

What had Hugo said? Something about being mated?

Maybe this was why I was acting so weird. Maybe it was all just some fated thing. I had heard about mates before. Certain species had various versions of a mating bond, but I didn't know a lot about it.

Well, if that was true, if I had some weird fated connection to a man that I knew nothing about and had no reason to have feelings for — well, I could see it being pretty rational that I had developed fondness for his cock, I guessed. Or his strands. I sucked in a breath at the thought of them and shivered in the memory.

Okay, but if I did have a fated connection and I was

out of control of myself, that was actually terrifying.

I liked Nich.

I had always liked Nich, since I was sixteen stars-shined years old.

For that feeling to be eclipsed right now by Hugo, it was… it was *against my will*.

This was all so fucked up.

I glared at the ceiling.

Even so… maybe my will was stupid and didn't know what was best for me. If I had some fated connection to Hugo, I owed myself to explore it, didn't I? What if he was my perfect match? What if we'd be insanely happy together? What if I let him go and I missed out on that?

I didn't think I'd sleep at all, but I must have, because the next thing I knew, Nich was shaking me awake.

"I got work later," he said. "I'm going to go home and find some breakfast, and if there's a cop-bot at my door, I'll key in the accident excuse and hopefully that'll work, and you won't have one at your apartment when you get there." Cop-bots were left behind when the police searched a place or investigated and couldn't find anyone. If the cop-bot could be assuaged, a case would be digitally closed as user error. Considering we hadn't just stayed where we were and waited to tell that to the actual police's faces was probably a problem, but hopefully Nich could get it off our backs.

If not, I just needed to stay clear of the police until I could pay off my debts, when I finally got access to my credits. Truth was, I was lucky that I'd been able to stay in my apartment as long as I had. Since I was on the debtors list and my address was a matter of public record, it was only bureaucracy that was keeping the wheels of justice from turning quickly enough to arrest me and throw me into a cell.

"Thanks," I said to him.

"You stay here until check-out time," he said. "You probably need your sleep."

"Hey," I said, "um... why didn't you ever see me that way?"

He furrowed his brow. "What do you mean?"

"I mean, I've been here, all these cycles," I said. "And you knew I wanted you, and you didn't want me back, but then... what? Why did it change?"

He squared his shoulders, looking uncomfortable. "I got work later."

"Not until after lunch hour, though, right? You have time. Don't you have time to talk? Just quickly? Just answer this."

"Why does this matter to you?"

Because I need to know if this is worth it, Nich, if I should give up my fated mate for you. "I just don't understand is all." I twisted my fingers in the blankets on the hotel room bed.

"Uh... well, it's kind of like I have boxes in my head, and I always put you in the little-sister box. I didn't think of you as having, like, sex, and then I *watched* you have sex, and it sort of forcibly ripped you out of that box and put you in the attractive-woman box."

"That's all?"

"Well, I thought... it's easy with us, right? We never argue. We hang out all the time. We've bailed each other out more than once, so we have each other's backs—"

"*You've* bailed *me* out, you mean," I said ruefully.

"I seem to remember someone pretending to be a nurse from the med center and calling in to my job to say that I was unable to work when I wanted to play hooky." He grinned at me.

I grinned back. "Yeah, I guess so."

"I just thought we were obviously perfect together. Like, uh, it would be easy. It would be good. And I still think that, but..."

"But?" I raised my eyebrows.

He spread his hands. "I think you're going to go after the gladiator."

"No," I said, too quickly. "No, I'm not going to do that. How would I even do that? I don't know how to find him."

"He was in your apartment. Your bracelet probably scanned his and put him in temporary contacts. I bet you can message him."

Right. I pressed my lips together and didn't meet his gaze.

"I get it," he said.

"I'm not going after him," I said. "It's like you said, he assaulted me."

"Yeah, you're pretty wrecked over it." Nich folded his arms over his chest.

"Well, it's confusing."

"I get that, too." He let out a little laugh. "I love you, Rowan. I care about you. I want you to be happy. We'd be happy together, but it would be a safe, comfortable kind of happy, and whatever that gladiator is, it's all angst and out-of-control yearning and adventure, and..." He chuckled ruefully. "I'm never going to compete with that."

My heart squeezed. "No, I'm not... you don't have to... it's not like that." I jumped out of the bed and went to him.

He backed away.

I put both of my hands on his chest. I'd never touched him like that.

He shook his head. "Don't."

"But Nich, I don't want you to feel like that. I don't want to… to hurt you."

"If I hadn't been stupid," he breathed, "and noticed you before, you never would have been in that arena."

"My father still would have died. There still would have been debts—"

"But I would have helped, and we could figured something out—"

"I wouldn't have let you—"

"If we were together, then your problems would be my problems. I would never have let you sell your body like that."

I tilted my head at him. "What's that in your voice?"

"Uh… I don't know?"

"You don't approve of what I did."

"Well, Rowan, no one would approve of that."

"But you got turned on by it, so turned on that now you want me, and yet you still—"

"That doesn't mean it was a healthy decision for you to have made."

"I didn't have a choice!"

"Of course you did. Stars, I would have helped you. If you had just come to me, I would have. And you could have gone elsewhere. The factory planets pay enough that if we both went, we could have worked it off in a couple years."

"I would never have let you do that," I said, shaking my head. "And I wouldn't work there either. That kind of work is brutal."

"I get the feeling you're picking a fight with me to make it easier on yourself when you choose him," he said. "You don't need to do that. I'm a big boy. I can handle rejection. And I *should* have noticed you before. Woman up, Rowan. Own it."

I scoffed. "That's not fair."

"I really… I have to work later, and I just want to get home and get some breakfast, okay? I don't want to talk anymore."

"Look, did you see that thing he typed? About being mated? Maybe it's just… against my will."

"Well, if it was really against your will, you'd be fighting it."

"Not if my will was… was taken over entirely."

He sighed. "Whatever, Rowan. You know, you *are* younger than me. Maybe our maturity levels about this —"

"Fuck you."

"I'm going," he said, turning his back on me.

My shoulders sagged. "I'm sorry, Nich. I didn't mean it."

"We'll talk later," he said with an air of finality, and then he was gone.

I went back over to the hotel room bed and flopped down face first in it. Why did this have to be so confusing? Why did it have to be so difficult?

* * *

hugo

I was in the middle of another disappointing visit to a ships dealer, because the credits I had were only going to be enough for some kind of clunker ship that would probably break down somewhere in the middle of deep space and leave me stranded, when my bracelet chirped at me.

I had a message.

I glanced at it, thinking again that I had *known* my

handler was going to screw me over.

It was from Rowan, and this stunned me. How did she have my contact information?

Can we meet somewhere to talk? it said.

"Anything important?" said the dealer in Cobran, who was a jeill, which meant that he had six spindly limbs around his segmented body. He was trying to show me some ship I couldn't afford. It was in better shape than the others, admittedly, and I liked it, but I couldn't buy this thing.

I eyed him shrewdly, an idea occurring to me. "Just something about another ship I'm looking into. Private sale from a current owner."

"If you do that, you're going to have to run all your documents yourself," said the dealer. "You'd be stuck planetside until they went through, and you'd never get clearance to take off. It could delay you for several suns. You buy from me, I'd have all that run in for you, and you could be leaving the atmosphere in eight hihors."

Inwardly, I smiled, because this was the first time the dealer had seemed the least bit concerned about my business. Maybe I could use this fictional sale that I'd made up. "Well, the price is a lot lower. What you're saying, the convenience, I agree that's worth paying a bit of a premium, but is there any way you can come down at all? I've got the credits, and I wouldn't need financing."

He rubbed two of his limbs together, thinking about it, and then he named a lower price.

I affected a pained expression. "I don't know. That's still a good bit higher than this other ship I'm looking at."

He named an even lower price.

"That I can do," I said, feeling vindicated.

As I was waiting in the dealership to sign paperwork and start the credit transfer, I considered the message from Rowan. I was honestly surprised, because I hadn't thought I would ever hear from her again. She obviously had a mate—at least she had some sort of male companionship in her life, and I could see from the territorial way he'd looked at me that he felt she was his.

I wasn't sure why she'd been in the ring with me, but maybe it was some kinky game between them.

Maybe they were in desperate financial straits or something.

And then there was the fact that I hadn't asked for permission before having sex with her again, which could be considered a crime. It happened amongst my people when mating bonds were being decided, but it was a different thing entirely when a woman understood what was happening. I thought the dynamic would change once a woman accepted the bond as well, but I couldn't be certain about that.

The mating madness in males continued until breeding was achieved. A male would sense, through the anchor strands, once the female was pregnant, and that would change the quality of the bond. Males remained bonded to females throughout pregnancy, but their arousal and sexual desires lost the violent intensity of the initial stages.

The bond tapered off after the young were born, and it typically didn't trigger again until the female had weaned their offspring. Our people tended to bond for life, so usually men triggered for the same woman again and again, but that wasn't necessarily always the case.

Given the biological nature of the mating madness, what I'd done to her hadn't strictly been in my control, and so I felt as if I'd been sort of assaulted as well, as if my own biological drives had had their way with both of us.

But I also felt guilty.

It wasn't my fault, not exactly, but it had been me that had done it.

I had been certain she would never want to see me ever again.

However, if she did want to talk, then I supposed I still owed her an explanation about what had happened. So, I messaged her back. *I might have some time this afternoon.*

Great. Somewhere public, okay? I'll give you the address of a diner near my place.

I considered. *I'm not sure my mating instinct is going to cooperate just because of social niceties. We should probably meet somewhere private.*

Nothing from her.

That was better. It wasn't fair to her to accept that being in each other's presence made me crazed.

My bracelet beeped. *Fine. My apartment then. When?*

Really?

I was stunned by that. Maybe I should find somewhere to go and rub one out before I saw her again. Would that make any difference?

Couldn't hurt.

* * *

rowan

I spent too much time getting ready for Hugo.

I changed my clothes five times even though he was probably just going to rip them off me. Considering that, though, I had to change again, into something that both looked good but that I didn't mind getting ruined.

I put my hair up and then took it down and then got it wet because it looked weird from being down and put product in it.

And then it was close to the time he was coming over, and I had wanted to put out some snacks on a tray, but I didn't have time now, and I also didn't have any matching cups clean, and I didn't know why I thought he would care if the cups matched, but I wanted to have matching cups for some reason.

When the entry query on the door sounded, I realized I hadn't really cleaned either, and that the place could have used it. I fluffed my pillows and artfully arranged my throw blanket, calling, "Just a hisec!"

However, when I opened the door, it was not Hugo there.

It was a cop-bot.

Stars! What was that doing here? When I'd gotten home, I hadn't found one, and I assumed that Nich had gotten them off our tail.

The cop-bot scanned me. "Rowan Llox, identity confirmed," it intoned.

I tried to shut the door.

It shot out two metal arms and pushed on the door, holding it open. "You are under arrest for unpaid debts. Do not attempt to pay now. Payment must be arranged through a court-appointed official during the hihors of 0700 and 1500 Starsday through Dustday—"

"Shut up," I said to the bot.

Which didn't listen but kept talking. It had cuffs.

I kicked the thing.

An alarm went off. "Do not resist arrest. Resisting arrest will result in force used to subdue the suspect.

Force may be deadly if deemed appropriate." The alarm continued to go off. "Please hold out your wrists for the scanner."

"I'm not letting you arrest me," I muttered. "I can pay the stupid debts."

"Do not attempt to pay now. Payment must be arranged—"

"Yeah, yeah, I got it," I said. I backed away from the bot and decided that I would barricade myself in my bedroom and try to figure out what I was going to do.

But then the bot followed me.

"Fuck you, bot!" I snarled at it.

Behind the bot, my door—encountering no resistance—snapped shut.

I hurled myself into my bedroom and shut that door.

The bot rolled into the door. "Do not evade arrest. Evading arrest can result in increased sentences of up to eight gemoons."

From outside my bedroom, I heard the query of the door.

Hugo!

"Hugo?" I yelled. "Is that you?"

There was no answer, and then my bracelet chirped that I had a message. I opened it.

Is something wrong?

I typed back. *Having a cop-bot problem.* Did he know what cop-bots were? I was guessing they didn't have them on Abbunia.

"Open the door, Rowan Llox. Your behavior is being logged and further charges may be filed if deemed appropriate," said the cop-bot.

What's that I hear in there? Hugo sent.

I can't let you in.

Do you want me to leave?

No.

Do you want me to break down your door?

Like that was nothing. He was really strong, wasn't he? I licked my lips.

Are you in danger?

I bet he'd be really protective of me in danger, like in a very hot and sweaty way. Stars, I had watched him kill men with his bare hands. I shivered.

I can smell your arousal through the walls.

He could what?

It's affecting the mating bond. I'm probably going to break down your door. Can't help it. Apologies.

There was a loud crashing noise, and the sound of buckling metal.

I tensed and then opened the door to my bedroom since I didn't necessarily want that broken too.

Hugo snarled through the apartment, picked up the cop-bot and ripped its metal limbs out of it, even as alarms sounded and the bot continued to scold and threaten legal action. Hugo picked the thing up and smashed it into the wall. He kicked it, and he was wearing boots, but I'd seen what he could do with his bare feet. The cop-bot didn't stand a chance.

In hidosecs, it was a sparking bit of twisted metal, lying on the floor.

Hugo's gaze met mine. He growled.

I panted. "Wait. Can you wait?"

He didn't wait. He pinned me to the wall next to my bedroom and put his mouth on my neck.

I sank my hands into the fur on his neck. It was kind of like a dark mane. It was soft. I liked it. "Does it have to… do you have to be inside me or do you just have to get off?"

He growled again. I was pretty sure those weren't

words, just out-of-control noises, but I didn't speak his language. He was working at my shirt. He was going to rip it.

I wriggled down between us, going down on my knees.

He tried to stop me.

I got my hand on his fly and opened that, and once I was stroking his thick hardness, he got pretty pliant. He made a wheezing noise, peering down at me.

I was eye-level with his cock, my hand wrapped around his girth. "I'm kind of sore anyway. This could be easier. Can you come quickly?"

He grunted.

The head of him was swollen and dark and glistening, weeping at me. I pumped him with my hand and he let out a whimper-groan.

His strands were floating around, seemingly confused.

I licked the head of him.

The strands suddenly connected to my face, all around my lips and down below my chin, over my throat.

I let out a surprised noise.

The strands were locked on, though, holding me in place.

Okay, then.

We were doing this. I eased my lips around his cock.

Unleashed, he drove himself into me, down my throat.

The strands pulsed into me, relaxing my muscles there. I didn't gag.

Instead, I took all of him, swallowed him easily. It felt... well, I'd always kind of liked giving blow jobs — maybe I just had a sensitive tongue or something, but if

I had the chance to rub my clit while I was doing it, it really turned me on, and I thought it felt good to have something in my mouth, too, just like kissing felt good.

This…

The position, how big he was, how wide my jaw was stretched, the feel of the head of him down my throat?

It was not exactly bad.

And when he started essentially fucking my mouth, thrusting into me, the strands sent a little pulse into me, and I felt it run up and down my body, lighting me up. My nipples hardened. My clit throbbed.

I couldn't form words, because he was down my throat. He stroked out enough for me to catch a breath through my nose, in an easy rhythm. I could probably groan, but talking was out of the question.

So, I silently sucked him, reveling in the sensation of it.

He looked down at me, one huge hand curled possessively around my jaw, and I locked my gaze with his as I took him and he claimed my mouth.

His strokes felt good, dark little glitters of something a bit forbidden. And looking into his eyes like this, it felt very intimate. My clit throbbed harder, and I didn't mind this in the least.

His breathing began to pick up speed, and I could tell he was getting close.

I was too. My clit gave me a little practice convulsion and then suddenly seized onto building pleasure. It took its cues from the rhythm of his strokes against my tongue. In, out, each stroke plunging me deeper into dark, wondrous goodness.

I came and he came right on the heels of me, and I swallowed him, my throat convulsing in time with both of our climaxes, and I felt as if I was borne up in the rush of dark water, waves of black-tinged froth breaking in my body again and again.

I panted.

He panted.

The strands pulsed into me, even as he was trying to detach, holding him there.

He growled an expletive, and brushed at them.

They tensed and then detached, and then he stumbled backwards, shaking his head, obviously annoyed with himself.

I wasn't. I got up and pressed myself into his chest and looked up at him, offering him my mouth. Would he kiss me after I'd just swallowed? Was he that kind of guy?

His expression softened when I was close. He gathered me into his arms, looking at me with wonder in his eyes. He uttered some sort of question.

I ran my fingers over one of his horns.

He put his mouth on mine. I opened my mouth for his tongue, and it swept inside.

I tangled my other hand into his mane again.

We kissed for a while.

NINE

hugo

I wasn't sure the strands were supposed to do that. I'd never seen them do that before.

I'd never...

Women in my clan didn't do things like that with their mouths, considering it couldn't possibly lead to children.

I'd heard of it, sure, but I'd never experienced it, and, uh...

Yeah, Rowan? She was *great*. Everything about her was perfection. I was currently kissing her like I couldn't get enough of her, and I never wanted to let go of her. I couldn't believe she'd willingly taken my cock into her mouth and swallowed me and that she had seemed to, well, could she have *enjoyed* that?

I knew that the bond had only joined us because of our biological potential for strong offspring, but I liked her. I liked *everything* about her.

I pulled away and stroked her pretty face, rubbing my fingers over her bottom lip. Her mouth was a little bit redder and her lips more full, and I thought about the way they'd looked wrapped around the base of me, and I was lost in a flood of emotion and awe.

"You're perfect," I said to her.

She gave me a grin, and the look on her face, was she

a little smitten too?

I pulled away, cringing. "Your boyfriend."

She reached for me. "What's wrong?"

Why couldn't we communicate?

I tried Cobran. "Do you speak Cobran?"

She recognized it. "No," she said in Cobran.

I laughed. What?

She switched to Common. "I can count to ten in Cobran, and say yes, no, and order food at Lanisson restaurants. But that's it."

I nodded. Of course. I got out my bracelet.

She lifted a finger. "Um, I want to talk. I have so many questions for you. But you destroyed a cop-bot?"

I looked down at the hunk of metal on the floor next to us. Oh, yeah, I had practically forgotten about that. When the mating madness was riding me, I didn't have control of my limbs. I was aware of what was going on, and sometimes I could sort of speak, but otherwise, I was like an animal, functioning entirely on instinct. It was actually sort of awful. I hated it.

"So, we should go, because if we don't go, more police will show up. With blasters. And they'll take me to debtors prison. Is there somewhere we can go?"

I *had* just purchased a ship.

* * *

hugo

Rowan was standing with her back to me at one of the consoles on the ship, fingers flying over the touch screen, and she couldn't see me even if I wanted to type something to her on my bracelet.

She suddenly gave a little jerk and then massaged her wrist under her bracelet. "Ouch," she said in Cobran. She turned to me, rubbing her temple. "Oh, that's a little like a brain freeze. Apparently, it only works on the ship, too. I never tried it before." She was still speaking Cobran.

I furrowed my brow.

"You know about this, right? It's a neural network. Sometimes there's a delay if the nets can't get the translation sent back to the receptors it puts in your brain?"

"You can speak Cobran," I said. "The ship did that?"

She laughed. "You're a little backward, aren't you? I like it. It's part of your charm."

"I'm a chieftain of an entire clan with a degree in agriculture and civics," I said, annoyed. I guessed the ship didn't have my clan's language as an option.

Her grin widened. "Oh, of course you are." She vaulted across the room to me. But then she stopped inches away from me. "If I touch you, are you going to go crazy and fuck me again? I mean, I don't entirely mind, but it *is* very interruptive."

"I think I'm getting a little accustomed to being around you. Or maybe my balls are empty. I did jerk off before I came to see you, not that it helped." Then I looked away, embarrassed. *Did I just say that out loud to her?*

"You wanting me so bad you can't control yourself? It's really hot," she said. "Kinda scary and also inconvenient, but... *hot.*"

I tried to find something to say back to that.

She was talking again. "If you have a double degree, why can't you speak Common?"

"I had a fever as a child that permanently damaged my vocal cords," I said.

"Oh!" She was concerned. Her small, pale hands fluttered around my neck.

This was affecting. I let out a labored breath.

Our gazes caught.

We stared at each other, not speaking for several long moments.

"Sorry," she whispered.

"Don't be," I said softly. "Nothing about you close is bad. But, um, you have a boyfriend, and—"

"Oh, no, I don't."

I lifted my chin. Really? "Does he know that?"

She laughed. "Yes."

"So, you're not… spoken for." My voice dipped in pitch.

She shook her head, smiling at me. "No. I mean… I don't know… Nich is…" She cocked her head, taking me in. "But you're so…" She sighed. "Can you tell me about this mating thing?"

"Certainly," I said. "I don't understand how it happened, honestly. I didn't think that I could bond to a human, but I did. I thought the bonds were only amongst my own species. My body will prepare at the sign of a potential mate, and my instinct can be triggered. But only after my strands have locked in does the bond become cemented on my part. I am bonded to you. I can only be aroused by you, not other women, and my body is very attuned to yours. When we're, um, copulating, I'm physically unable to climax unless you do, for instance, and the strands give me information about how to please you. I can't exactly feel what you're feeling, but I have a sense of it."

She gaped at me. "Whoa." She put a small palm on my chest. "That's… hot."

I couldn't help but smile a little. "But you haven't accepted the bond, so if you don't want it, as long as we're separated, my connection to you will wear off, and nothing at all has happened to your body, so don't worry."

"Oh." She drew back. "I'm not bonded to you?"

"Not yet. You'd have to accept it."

"So, everything I'm feeling, it's all me?"

I was confused. "Who else would it be?"

She took two steps away from me. She turned her back and looked down at her shoes.

"Rowan? Are you all right?"

"I just… I thought… the way I react to you, I've never felt anything like it."

That went through me, and my body reacted. I felt it in my chest and then an echo of it in my groin. But my cock only half-hardened and my madness didn't trigger, and I let out a relieved breath.

She turned and gave me a shy smile. "I thought maybe… maybe it was like fate or something."

"The bond isn't fate," I said. "It's biology. It's purely a function of physicality. It doesn't mean we'd be a good fit personality-wise or anything."

"Oh," she said.

"I mean, I like you. I think… I feel as though we'd… I came to ask you to come with me to my planet, to be my mate, to be my chieftess."

Her mouth opened very wide and then she shut it. "Like a queen? I go with you and accept the bond and then I'd be a Treebark person queen?"

I nodded, smiling at her. "Yes."

"And have your half-Abbunian babies?"

"Yes." My voice had no bottom. The thought of her pregnant with my young seemed to have stolen it.

"Whoa," she said. Her voice wasn't strong either.

"I know it's crazy," I said. "But if I've bonded to you, even if it isn't fate, it does mean something about the two of us together. And the, uh, the sex thus far is, uh, well, I've never felt anything like—"

"Me either," she said, coming closer to me. "Your strands, they're… I *like* those strands. And your cock, it also… I like that too."

"It likes you," I rumbled, and now, roots and branches, I was getting harder. I wanted to reach for her, but I backed up, drawing in several breaths.

"I like looking at it, and licking it—"

"Stop," I ground out.

"Oh." She backed up. "Is that getting you going?"

I didn't answer, concentrating on taking long, calming deep breaths, thinking about very unsexy things.

"Sorry," she said quietly.

I just breathed. I could feel the madness at the bottom of my spine, and I concentrated on relaxing and feeling it ebb out, like a muscle that was no longer contracting. Well. That was apparently possible. I wondered if I could do it again.

Finally, I raised my gaze to hers. "All right, I think I'm okay."

"You, um, stopped it that time?"

"I did," I said. "I don't know if I could do it again. I'm not sure why it's different this time."

"Maybe it's your general level of stress," she said, shrugging. "I mean, every other time, things have been a little heightened, but we're in the middle of a regular conversation, so maybe that makes a difference?"

It was as good a theory as any. If she stuck around, I guessed I'd have to test it.

"Does it change if I accept the bond?" she said.

"Yes," I said. Then I thought about the fact that mated pairs in my clan usually went off for their noccht—an extended stretch of time somewhere away from everyone else so that they could have round-the-clock sex. "Sort of."

"Sort of?"

"I know it gets less violent once you're pregnant." I winced. "I mean, once the female is pregnant."

"Okay," she said. "And, uh, how do I accept this mating bond?"

"Well, the female marks the male," I said. I touched my shoulder. "Usually here."

"Marks?"

"With her teeth."

"You mean bites."

I squinted at her. "You don't have teeth like my people have teeth."

She ran her tongue self-consciously over her teeth. "That's really… intense."

I stepped closer to her. I put my fingers on her chin so that I could inspect her mouth.

She let me.

"It's got to be possible for you to accept the bond, or I wouldn't have bonded to you already," I murmured.

"I could use something, maybe, like a knife." She made a face. "But… I don't know."

"I think the saliva's important," I said. "That signals something in my body to change the quality of the bond. I think it affects the signals the strands receive from you as well."

"So, I could cut you and spit in it." She let out a nervous laugh. "This is sounding really romantic."

"Are you considering this?" I was really shocked by that, I had to say. I was glad, but I didn't understand it. "If you come with me, you'd be leaving everything behind."

"I don't have anything to leave," she said. "My

parents are both dead, and I don't have any other family. There's Nich, but... I mean, sometimes we go moons without even messaging." Then, she gave me an embarrassed look. "Sorry, I don't mean to sound so pathetic."

"Nothing about you seems pathetic to me," I said. I drew in a breath. "But I guess I must have known you must be having a difficult time if you signed up to be a gladiator's prize."

She swallowed. "You, um, think less of me because of that?"

"That would be hypocritical of me, wouldn't it?"

She smiled. "I want to do it. I want to accept the bond."

"Really?" I couldn't help but smile at her.

"Yeah." She nodded. "Should I try to bite you?" She let out a little laugh, her cheeks reddening. She stepped closer, hands going to the collar of my shirt. "Would it be easier to take this off?"

Oh, she was close. I peered down at her, feeling a little lightheaded. "Right now?" I said huskily. "Don't you want to think about it?"

She shook her head. "No. I want this. It's an adventure. And I want you. And to be a queen and to have babies and a family. I want... to matter to someone, you know?" Her voice cracked and she hid her face, embarrassed.

I lifted her face, looking at her.

"Sorry, that was pathetic again," she said quietly.

"No," I said. I kissed her. "You matter to me."

She sagged into me, her soft body against mine.

I wrapped my arm around her waist to support her. "If you do this, you're going to be the most important person to me in the universe. You're going to matter a lot. We're going to matter to each other."

She touched my face. "You make me feel…"

"What?"

"Everything," she said. "Just… sexy and pretty and interesting and… and *everything*. I'd be stupid not to take a chance on this. I'd regret it for the rest of my life."

I got a strange feeling she was trying to convince herself of this. "If you want to think it over —"

"Think it over where?" She brushed her fingertips over one of my horns. "I can't go back to my apartment. The cop-bots have found me, and now I've probably got a list of charges as long as my arm in addition to the debts."

"Right, why don't you tell me about that?" I said. "Why are you having issues with the law?"

"It's not like *that*." She pulled away from me, twisting her fingers together.

"I don't have any respect for authority in this Toth-controlled universe," I muttered. "You don't have to feel ashamed."

She looked up at me, gratefulness all over her face. "Okay, well, my dad, he used to gamble a lot. Betting on gladiator fights mostly. When I was younger and still living with him, it could get really bad. Sometimes, he would lose so much money that they turned off the heating elements in the apartment or we couldn't afford food. Anyway, when he died, I…" She shook her head, looking disgusted with herself. "It was dumb. I had this stupid burst of sentimentality. I mean… he wasn't winning any awards for his fathering, *ever*, but he was dead, and I didn't want him just disintegrated and dispersed into space. I wanted to have his dust and to have a plaque in one of the cemeteries, you know, just a place to go and remember him or something? So, I claimed him and did the paperwork for next of kin. But it was dumb, because then I found out there was no money for a plaque or an urn or anything, and that now I was on the hook for all of his debts."

I nodded slowly.

"If I'd just let him go, if I hadn't had that moment of stupid sentimentality—"

"You're blaming yourself for that?" I said softly. "Really?"

"Well, if I hadn't—"

"I think sometimes it's hard to accept that life is simply unfortunate a lot of the time," I said. "I used to think that it was somehow my fault for the fact I was in a gladiator contract. Maybe somehow when I was at university, I got the Treebark people on the Toth's radar, or something?"

"No, you know they just pick planets randomly and—"

"Exactly." I nodded. "Randomly. And the fights, they're really as much about chance as skill. My last one, I was two inches from falling to my death."

"I know." She drew herself up. "I was terrified." She stepped close to me again. "Hugo, I felt connected to you right away. Even from just looking at your holopic."

"Me too," I breathed.

"Doesn't that mean something? Don't you think?"

The point I had just been about to make was that nothing meant anything and that we were playthings of cruel forces bigger than ourselves, tossed about between the stars to live or die at the whim of things we had no control over, caught in a series of random coincidences, and that her own pain was not her fault, because bad things just happened all the time. For no reason.

But…

"I do," I whispered. "I think it does mean something." I kissed her again.

She plastered her body against mine, and we stroked our tongues against each other, and she felt perfect in my arms, as though her body belonged right here, as though we had been designed to fit together.

She pulled away, gasping. "Your *tongue*."

I let out a little laugh.

"It's good," she said.

"I like yours too." I put my thumb in her mouth to touch it. It was small and thick and pink. Everything about her was sort of small and soft and pale, and I approved of all of it.

She sucked on my thumb.

I grunted.

The mating instinct roared again, traveling up my spine. I gasped and tried to pull my finger out of her mouth.

She didn't let me. She bit down on me.

I panted, locking my gaze with hers.

I lost any control over the mating madness as her teeth bore down, hard, and I felt pain as they broke my skin.

I convulsed.

She ran that little pink tongue of hers over the wound she'd created.

I shut my eyes, shaking all over.

The mating madness surged, taking over me.

I picked her up. She was small and she didn't weigh very much.

She wrapped her legs around my hips.

I ripped her clothing to get at her, and I felt the wound in my finger pulse and then I... it was very strange, but it was like I was in two places at once. I was inside my body, but I could feel the sensations in her body as well.

Her body was dimmer, a shadow or an echo, not as bright as my own, but I could sense her. She was eager and excited, but not truly aroused, because I could sense that her kind needed time to become fully aroused.

This was what I wanted to do with her. I wanted to spread her out and take my time to lick her and taste her. I had wanted this since the beginning, and the mating madness wasn't letting us do that—what would be better for both of us.

I thought this through a haze, even as I pressed her into a wall, bracing her there, even as her fingers were working at unfastening my fly.

My strands brushed against her fingers.

She was still sucking my thumb, which was still bleeding into her mouth, and she moaned around it.

"I'm so sorry it keeps doing this to us," I breathed into her ear. "I want this slower."

She only moaned in response.

One of my strands locked into her body, and she jolted.

I felt it from inside her, felt the way it vibrated through her sensitive places, and it made me crazy. My cock was mostly hard, but now it throbbed and thickened and hardened. It pushed against her pussy, and she wasn't wet enough for me and the strands knew it and I knew it, and—if I had any control—we'd back this up and slow this down—but instead, my strands sent information to my cock, which expelled enough of a viscous liquid to ease my entry, and I speared her, sinking into her.

She cried out, opening her mouth around my thumb.

I felt that I hurt her, even as my strands altered her muscles, easing her discomfort.

"I'm sorry," I said again.

"It's okay, it's okay, it's good." Her voice was thick and full of pleasure.

"I can feel that it hurts you."

"It doesn't hurt *now*."

I could feel that was true too, as I started to thrust into her. "I just… I want… I want to feel like *we're* having sex, not that it's having us."

She laughed a little, sweet little tongue lapping at my thumb again. "I feel you too."

"Do you?"

"Stars, your cock likes my pussy, doesn't it?" She giggled.

"Yes," I said, because she felt like tight, warm velvet, and I loved being buried in her.

"Make me come, Hugo," she said. "Use your strands and make me come all over your thick cock. Please."

I grunted, and my strands went deeper into her, and she wriggled into me. We moved together.

"You can't come until I do?" she asked me.

"No," I said.

She shivered. Suddenly, she bit down on my thumb again, breaking the skin again.

I jerked against her, going rigid and then doubling my speed as I started to pound her pussy relentlessly. The extra wound opened our bond wider, and I felt her more intensely.

"Fuck," she mumbled around my thumb, clutching at me, her breath coming in high-pitched sounds that sounded almost like sobs. "Fuck, I can really feel you now."

"Yeah," I said.

"And this all feels so good," she groaned. "I never felt anything—Stars—Fuck."

My body was tight and flush with goodness, but it was all held in check, in service to her. It felt great, but there was no hint of a climax, none except hers, which I could feel her chasing, the edge of it rushing toward her body like an approaching meteor.

Instinctively, my strands altered and I shifted the position of my cock. I felt the head change shape, and I felt it when I slid home in the spot that massaged the inside of her clitoris.

She made another sob-cry.

I fucked her.

Her mouth fell open.

I spread my bloody thumb over her bottom lip, smearing myself all over her skin.

The meteor crashed into her.

She came.

We came.

It was heat and light and fire and it ignited and destroyed us both.

TEN

Hugo's cock was still inside me, but it was growing soft.

We were still against the wall. I had my legs wrapped around him. He was half-collapsed into me, bracing himself with one arm so that his weight wasn't fully against me.

I was touching his horn, and then idly rubbing my fingers over his face. It was so nice how close I felt to him right now, how I had this sense of his body. It wasn't overwhelming, but I could feel what he felt, and it had made my orgasm three times as intense, his pleasure weaving its way through mine, and that sensation I'd had in the ring — that I couldn't tell where I began and he ended? It was so much more overwhelming now, so much better. I loved it.

"I guess I accepted the bond," I said.

"Yeah." He gave me a smile, and it was so threaded with affection and familiarity that I shivered a little. "I'm glad."

"Me too," I breathed. "Is it bad that I didn't mark your shoulder, though? Is that something that your people are going to look for?" Maybe it was like a wedding ring. My parents had them. It was an Earth thing, and not even every part of Earth, just certain

109

cultures did it, but apparently on some parts of Earth, you could just look and see if a person had a ring on a certain finger and then you'd know that person was taken.

"We can fix that later," he said. "Don't worry about that. And maybe it doesn't matter. This is going to be a different sort of mating, considering you're human and I'm not."

I felt a tinge of apprehension. "Is that going to be bad?"

"Nothing about you is even close to being bad. You're wonderful and amazing and perfect." His voice had gone a little hoarse.

I wrapped my hand around his horn. "You're kind of perfect yourself."

He gently eased my legs down to the floor and his cock slid out of me.

I whimpered. "I like you inside me."

"I'm going to be inside you a lot of the time," he said. "You're sore, though. I've injured you. It's because of the mating madness. It's… it's not ideal for human anatomy. I could sense you need more time to become fully aroused."

"I, um, get fully aroused, trust me." I sagged against the wall, toes curling.

"It forces it," he said. "But I think it could damage you if we're not careful." He gave me a very serious look. "The last thing I want is you damaged."

"I don't want damaged either." I put my hand on his chest. "But I'm fine, Hugo. I'm okay."

"It's my job to protect you," he said. "Even if that means protecting you from myself."

I liked that. I dragged my hand over his chest. "So… here's the thing. I need to stay on Kalion until tomorrow until my account will let me withdraw credits and pay off my debts. I probably have fines too." Thinking of that dampened my good mood. "So, can you stay docked here until then? If you can't, we could probably just orbit until tomorrow? Then we can go to Abbunia, as soon as that's done."

"Oh," he said. "You don't need to say goodbye to anyone?"

"I told you, there's no one."

"I still don't understand about that man who was in your apartment, who's not your boyfriend."

"Well…" I grimaced. "That's all just complicated." I really didn't like deliberating over making decisions, and I didn't know what to do about Nich. Now, it was just sort of decided. I was mated. End of story.

Sometimes, I was a little impulsive.

"You want to talk about it?"

"I'll send him a message or something," I said. Nich had indicated that he knew I was going to choose Hugo anyway. Still, I felt guilty.

"You're regretting it," he said. "You're regretting accepting the bond."

"Stars, no!" I shook my head at him.

"It's only that we barely know each other, and I told you this is all just physical, and…"

"*You're* regretting it," I said, and it was like I'd been doused in cold water.

"No." He shook his head firmly.

We both eyed each other.

Then we both looked away.

Stars, sometimes I was so *stupid*. I didn't mean to be. I really didn't. I guess nobody means to do stupid things, really, but sometimes I felt like I was the stupidest person in the history of the universe. The first time I'd thrown myself at Nich, for instance? That had been stupid too.

I should have known that if Nich actually had feelings for me, he would have shown them at some point, and that telling him I was into him shouldn't have been necessary. I'd even had that exact conversation with myself about him, and then, somehow, we'd been together, and it had just popped out of my mouth unbidden.

It was like biting Hugo's thumb.

It just… happened.

I must have decided to do it, but now that it was done, it didn't feel like I had.

"What?" said Hugo. "What are you thinking?"

I shrugged. "Nothing. Do you mind sticking around Kalion until tomorrow?"

"Of course not. If you need to stay longer, we can."

"You want to get out of here? Go out somewhere and get a few drinks or something? Dance?"

"I thought you were wanted by the law."

"Yeah, they'll send another bot to my apartment probably." I shrugged. "Truthfully, the law is kind of corrupt around here. There's a lot of organized crime infiltrating it. That's why they can put people in jail for debt and stuff."

He nodded, as if this was typical. "Of course."

"But if we go out somewhere, it should be fine." I smiled at him.

"And that's what you want to do." He eyed me.

I nodded. "Definitely." I kind of wanted to run. I wanted us to just blast off from the planet right now and leave all this behind. Since I couldn't do that—I wouldn't be able to do credit transfers from deep space, and I wasn't sure what the situation was on Hugo's home planet in terms of connecting to the galactic nets—going out dancing was the next best thing.

"Well, if that's what my mate wants." His lips curved into a smile. "Then let's do that. I want to make you happy, Rowan."

My stomach did a flip-flop. Okay, maybe I wasn't stupid after all. Maybe this was going to all work out just fine.

* * *

hugo

I'd ruined Rowan's clothes, and she couldn't go back to her apartment for more, so she sent me. We communicated about this via bracelet as I gathered everything and packed it up, and I evaluated what kind of a team we were.

She was pretty great at dictating to me what she wanted me to do, which was good, because I took direction fairly well. I thought packing a woman's clothes for her had a ninety percent chance of being disastrous, but it went surprisingly well, so I thought that boded well for our future.

Then she changed and we went out to a club in the middle of the afternoon and she promptly started drinking alcohol and I did too.

Honestly, I hadn't had a chance to do something like that since before being a gladiator, and at first, it was good.

I enjoyed the way that alcohol made me feel a little fuzzy around all my edges, how it was pleasant, and we danced together on the mostly-empty dance floor. We couldn't talk to each other outside of the ship, because she needed the ship to handle the translation, but that didn't seem to be a problem, because we didn't need to talk to dance.

But then two things happened.

One was that people recognized us, which shouldn't have been a surprise, since my fight had been broadcast, and since this planet—so close to the big arena—was pretty tuned in to the gladiator fights.

And the other was that my mating instinct triggered.

I thought I might have fought it down, but I couldn't, because I was so bonded to her that I could feel her, and she was pretty turned on by all of the people knowing who we were and with them all watching us.

I managed to get us out of the bar and into a small alley before I lost it, but half the bar came too, and so there we were, her clutching the wall, back arched, ass up, me behind her, and the sex was fast and furious and… and *good*.

Of course it was good.

It was always good with her, and she got off really fast with all the eyes on her, and I thought there was a *reason* she'd signed up to get fucked in the middle of an arena, and I wondered what the roots I had gotten myself into.

I mean, it shouldn't have mattered, because all those people had already watched me fuck her. They'd seen our first time, you know, and fucking her in that dirty, dark alley was *hot*, and her pussy was warm and eager, clamped around my cock, gripping me as I rammed her from behind, and when I came, I felt like my entire body cracked in half and fell to the ground to shatter into fine pieces of dust. Which all came back together and then exploded again and again and *again*. I felt her climax and mine and I was unmade by all of it.

But…

That thing in the arena, *it* was assault.

It was done *to* us.

I guessed I had some unexamined trauma about that entire chapter of my life. Probably, in a perfect world, I should have gone home to Abbunia, tried to work through that, tried to return to my position ruling my people and simply adjusted to *not* being a gladiator.

Probably in a perfect world, starting a very intense relationship with a virtual stranger was…

Yeah, even in a less-than-perfect world, that was a terrible idea.

The thing was that I was falling for this woman. Yeah, I sensed that she was actually not perfect, because no one was perfect, and that she had some unresolved trauma too. Her father sounded like… well, I was glad the guy was already dead, because otherwise I might have wanted to kill him myself.

I desperately wanted to protect her.

I wanted to somehow go back and protect her in the past, to go and fix all those things that had traumatized her.

And I would never be able to do that.

So, here we were, two possibly super fucked-up people *mated*, and I was feeling my entire being align to her. She was becoming astonishingly important to me. But the problem was, I had an entire clan at home to whom I was responsible and I wasn't sure how well she was going to mesh with that kind of responsibility.

I was a little anxious about the future.

Then the not-boyfriend showed up.

While I was tucking away my dick and she was surveying her pants, which were ripped, because of my lack of control during the mating bond. I was not sure it was wise for us to be in public like this when I was obviously some kind of sex-crazed savage around her.

While we were still sticky and sweaty and both smelling of sex, the not-boyfriend, who was named Nich, I seemed to remember, came through the gathered crowd and looked at both of us with violence in his eyes.

Now, I really wished I could communicate. I wished I could talk to this guy. He was obviously into her, and he'd be jealous and hurt regardless, but if I could talk, I could try to explain that I would never hurt her, and that I cared about her, that I was falling in love with her. That might help ease his concern.

I took off my shirt.

Nich's nostrils flared.

But I just handed it to Rowan, gesturing she could tie it around her waist to cover herself.

"Thanks, Hugo," she said. "Maybe going out in public was stupid. I keep forgetting about what this bond does to us."

Was that the truth? She'd enjoyed it a lot. To be fair, I had too. Voyeurism was not my thing, but sex with her was indescribably amazing, so it had overridden any discomfort I might have felt.

Nich folded his arms over his chest. "Thanks for ignoring all my messages, Rowan."

She wasn't looking at him. "A cop-bot came to my apartment and —"

"Yeah, I went by. I saw the door. I was really worried about you." He looked me up and down.

I met his gaze. I tried not to challenge him with my look, but I wasn't going to look away and be ashamed either.

"But I see you didn't waste time," he said. He shook his head. "You know… I don't know why I didn't realize, but that arena thing is *exactly* like you. It's completely what you would do." He was looking at me as he was saying this, but talking to Rowan. "I mean, there was that time you called me because you danced on the table at that bar, and you were terrified of that guy—"

"You said that wasn't my fault," said Rowan. "You said that no matter how sexy I danced, that guy shouldn't have thought he was owed anything from me."

"He was a gratts, yes," said Nich, turning to look at her. "But you…"

"What?" She lifted her chin. "You disapprove of me."

"I worry about you."

"We would never have worked."

"Maybe not. I think you need more than someone like me could ever give you," said Nich. He turned back to me. "I hope you're enough for her. I hope you make her happy."

"He does," said Rowan, stepping closer to me, putting a hand on my bare chest. "He really does. And we're leaving in the morning."

"Leaving?" said Nich.

"We have to go back to Hugo's clan on Abbunia," she said. "He's the chieftain. I'm his chieftess."

Nich let out a laugh.

"What?"

"No, nothing. Of course you need to be a chieftess." He lifted both of his hands. "You need to fuck for an audience, and you need a clan."

I decided I didn't like his tone. I took a step toward him.

He held up his hands, warding me off. "We're cool, gladiator guy. We're very cool. Don't worry, I've never touched her. She's all yours." He turned back to Rowan. "Were you even going to say goodbye to me? No matter what all this is, you were always like family to me, ever since Jeffi died."

"Of course I was!" Rowan was defensive. She lurched forward and hugged Nich hard. "I'm going to miss you. You're… I mean…" She pulled back. "Thank you for everything, and I promise to keep in touch and…" She bit down on her lip. "I think this could be good for me, Nich, can you try to be happy for me?"

His voice softened. "Yeah, of course I am." He glanced at me. "Does he… talk?"

"He has a speech impediment," she said. "Or something. I guess I don't really know what a speech impediment is." She looked up at me.

I shrugged. It sounded right to me.

"He speaks Cobran," she said. "He can't pronounce Common with his vocal cords."

"So, he's, uh, he's intelligent?"

I growled at him.

"He has a double degree in agriculture and civics." She drew herself up.

I had to grin at how defensive she was of me. It made me want to kiss her.

"Okay." Nich put both of his hands up again. "Sorry." He looked at me. "Sorry, man. Just, uh, be good to her. She's… she's got a really good heart, and she hasn't had an easy life."

"Nich, don't," she said.

"I'll be good to her," I said in Cobran, putting my arm around her. "You can count on that."

He didn't seem to understand exactly, but he got the gist. He nodded.

After that, we went back to the ship, where we could

talk.

She was embarrassed and apologetic, but I tried to reassure her it was going to be okay. I thought about explaining to her that I wasn't sure that I was particularly into the voyeuristic thing, but then I decided it didn't matter.

It wasn't going to be a problem on Abbunia.

It was going to take us half a gemoon to get there anyway. With any luck, I might have her pregnant before we got there, and then the bond would calm down.

And if she wasn't pregnant, we'd be able to go away together, like newly mated couples did, and we'd be alone to indulge until that did happen. No one would bother us, and there would be no groups of people to fuck in front of.

Besides, it wasn't as if I hadn't enjoyed it. Maybe it was a thing I could do occasionally for her if she wanted it.

I just… I would have to work through the association I had with the arena, with the fights, with…

No, I didn't want to think about that.

It was over.

I was free.

ELEVEN

The next morning, I sat in the common lounge on Hugo's ship, clicking through on my bracelet and setting up transfers. Even though I knew I was going to have to do it, I had a sinking sensation in my stomach as I watched the balance shrink, watched all the money go right back out the door the hisec it had come in.

It was crazy to me that all of this was so easily done, that if I'd had money, these debts would have been nothing, but that I'd had to tear my life apart because of them.

Of course, maybe it had all worked out for the best.

I also had set up a transfer to pay back Nich for that hotel room he'd gotten for us. There was a spot to type out a message to accompany the transfer of credits, but I hadn't been able to think of anything else to say to him, so I'd left it blank.

Hugo sauntered into the room. He had gone out for food for us. He set the bags on the table, and I noticed there was a little gleaming metal device attached around his ear. "What's that?"

A voice answered me in Common. "I used to have one before I was a gladiator. I thought I should see if I could afford another one, and I had enough credits leftover from buying the ship to get it. I guess I negotiated my handler to give me just enough." It was Hugo's voice, and it had his inflections, but it was also digital. It sounded a little like a bot.

I grinned. "But I can speak Cobran," I said in Cobran.

"Only on the ship," he said. "When we get to Abbunia, we'll need another solution."

"I'm going to learn your language," I said. "If I'm going to be the Treebark chieftess, I need to speak the language."

He grinned at me. "I have no doubt you will learn it, but I imagine that might take some time. Until then, we have some communication options."

I furrowed my brow. "Wait, your handler gave you money for the ship? Why were you able to access it right away instead of having to wait two business suns?"

"I guess because it was a Toth-created account," he said with a shrug.

"Oh, right," I said. I started to take food out of the bag he'd brought.

"How's your debt-paying going?"

"Almost done," I said.

"Does it feel good, knowing that's off your back, especially after everything you had to go through to get the money?"

I glanced at him. There was something in his tone that I wasn't sure how to take. "You said it would be hypocritical of you to judge me for the arena."

He tilted his head in confusion. "I don't judge you. It *would* be hypocritical. I had to do it too. I understand that you had no real choice."

Maybe I was imagining things. "I thought it would be awful, but I'm glad it was you, and that it was so amazing."

He eyed me. "And the added bonus of how arousing it was to know everyone was watching?"

"What?" I went back to the food, shaking my head. That was not why I did it. Definitely not.

Sometimes, I had to admit that I did feel… I don't know… invisible. Like no one saw me, and no one cared, and that I didn't matter.

And maybe… maybe something about the arena had felt…

"Nothing," said Hugo. "I don't know why I said that."

I raised my gaze to his.

"Let's just eat," he said, taking the food containers out. "We can talk about Abbunia instead. You don't know anything about it, I imagine."

"Um, no," I said. This part of the galaxy was littered with planets that supported life and almost all of them had various different species on them. It would be impossible to keep track of all of them. "I want to know everything. What's the climate like?" My planet Kalion was covered primarily in water, and there were only a few small land masses that were inhabitable. There were larger ones around the southern pole of the planet, but it was punishingly cold there and so no one lived there.

"It's a fairly cold climate," he said. "Most of the settlements are concentrated around the equator, which is a mild sort of temperature year round. Not too hot, but we can grow crops year round, and there are a lot of trees."

"Well, I kind of figured." I took a bite of breakfast. "You being Treebark people and all."

"Further north or south of the equator on Abbunia,

the temperature can quickly become far too cold to support life. There are two large cities on the equator, but my people live in a rural area."

"I figured that too," I said.

"Well, maybe you should tell me what you suspect, and I'll tell you where you're right and where you're mistaken?" He smiled at me. "Or do you want to ask questions?"

I tried to think of what I might want to ask, but it was overwhelming, because there was so much to think about. And I actually didn't really suspect much at all. I wasn't in a position to know much about his culture or people. "How much technology do you have?"

"As much as anyone," he said, giving me a look.

"Sorry!" I said. "You said you're a chieftain, and I know that the Toth come to planets where the technology is low —"

"Look, we were primitive, but that was three generations ago. My parents grew up knowing about the wide universe and flying ships and my father went to university. So, there's definitely a clash there between the old ways and the new ways, but that doesn't mean we're backward or something."

"I didn't mean anything by it," I said, because I could hear defensiveness in his tone.

"No, I know that," he said, a little chagrined. "Just because we've moved into the galactic society doesn't mean we've got the money or the weapons to fight the Toth if they decide to show up. I did the best I could with that contract. Maybe if my father had still been alive — but no, they just would have taken him instead of me."

"Oh, I didn't know about your father," I said. "I'm so sorry."

"It was a long time ago." He raised his eyebrows. "And I could hardly be a chieftain if my father was alive."

"So, it's hereditary, this ruler thing?"

He sighed.

Before the Toth had risen up, there had been a more egalitarian, democratic government in place, though most of it was in the form of a set of rules that everyone had adopted and followed. It was kind of like the United Nations or something. Not that I knew about that either, exactly, but this was how it was explained to me as a kid. My parents talked about Earth stuff a lot when I was a kid, but they only knew about it second hand, having never been to Earth either. The Toth paid lip service to democratic ideas, but only Toth were allowed to have a say in government, and they made rules that only benefited their race.

I tried to walk this whole conversation back. "I mean, I was basically just asking because I wanted to know if there would be hot showers and toilet facilities." Which, really, this was a thing I hadn't thought to ask before accepting the mating bond? I *was* stupid.

He put one meaty finger down on the table. "Yes, we have an inherited governmental structure, but it's primarily ceremonial these days, because we're all being ruled by the Toth, so no government we put in place would have any power. But also, we're not a rich people, and I was the only member of my clan who was able to travel, to get a degree, to learn about the galaxy. So, it's only natural that I'd be the best qualified to make these kinds of decisions for my people. And it's not… it's not like you're thinking. It's a responsibility, it's a burden, it's not… power or something. I have to take care of them and they need me. The whole reason I went into the ring was for my people, and—"

"I know," I said. "Of course it was." I remembered what he'd said to be about how his job was to protect me, and even though I didn't know Hugo very well, I could see what kind of man he was, and he was a good man. "I really didn't mean anything by it."

He looked me over. He hung his head, running his hand through the mane that grew on the back of his neck. "I'm being a little defensive."

"No, it's understandable," I said. "I wasn't thinking about it from your perspective. I could have put myself in your place before I said the things I said."

He lifted his gaze to mine. "Well, I could have been thinking more of your perspective, which is leaving everything you know all for me, and you know nothing about where you're going. You're just asking for information, and I've got a chip on my shoulder."

"I'm sure you have a good reason for that."

He shrugged. "At university, I was definitely idiotic about everything. I was the backwoods primitive Abbunian. And then I've spent years of my life being treated essentially like an animal, like a possession. So, I guess… is that a good reason?"

"Yes." I reached out and put my hand on his. My heart lurched painfully at that description of himself, though I knew it was accurate when it came to the Toth. "I'm sorry."

"Me too," he said, twisting his fingers with mine.

I looked down at our fingers. There, our digits entwined, we didn't look like different species.

"Hey," he said in a low voice, "maybe this is going to be fine."

"This? What?"

"I mean, you and me, mating like this, being crazy with each other, when we barely know each other? As long as we can communicate and empathize with each other, we can do this. I think we got through that just fine."

"We did." I smiled at him, squeezing his fingers with mine.

His expression changed as he looked at me. It grew very tender.

My lips parted. I *liked* Hugo. *Really* liked him. He was *very* likable.

"There are showers," he said in a soft voice, giving me a little smile.

I laughed. "Good to know."

He leaned across the table and kissed me.

I shut my eyes, realizing we'd never kissed like this. It had always been intense, passionate kisses that seemed to overtake us. This was sweet and slow and soft, just our lips meeting.

We pulled away, and he had a silly grin on his face, and I knew I had a matching one.

Oh, I was definitely in the throes of first infatuation here, which was good. Maybe I'd wanted the mating bond to decide everything for me, and to make it full-on love, but this was actually better, that it was growing a little more slowly.

"What you're saying about it being a responsibility?" I said. "If I'm your chieftess, that'll be my responsibility too. So, what do your people need? What will I do for them?"

He let out a noisy, affected breath and then kissed me again, harder. He let go of my hand to cup my face with both of his palms. When he pulled back, I was breathless.

"What was that for?" I managed.

"You're amazing that you would say that," he said. "You get it. I think you're going to be a wonderful chieftess."

I smiled, but I was confused. "What did I say? I just asked a question."

"You asked what you need to do for them, though," he said. "Your, uh, that Nich guy, he was rude to you. He made it sound like you were doing all this for shallow reasons, like you were doing it because you wanted to be admired or worshiped or something. But if that were the case, you would have asked what they would do for *you*, not what you would do for *them*."

I shrugged, feeling a little embarrassed. I hadn't thought about it like that. And it made me feel good what he was saying, but I had to admit, I had been drawn to the idea of being his queen, and not exactly because I had thought of it as a service profession. What if I screwed this up? "So, what *do* I do?"

He shook his head. "You don't need to worry. Like I said, it's mostly a ceremonial position at this point. Occasionally, maybe I arbitrate disputes if they can't work things out on their own, and I'd value your perspective on that, but... we're not riding to war with other clans or something."

I laughed again, but it was a nervous laugh. I'd never considered war.

"When we get to Abbunia, my mother will help you," he said.

"Right," I said. He had a family. Of course he did. Would they like me? "Have you told your mother about me?"

"There hasn't been time," he said. "But before we take off, I guess I'll send a message to let them know

I'm on my way home and I'll let them know about you as well."

"Do you have brothers and sisters?"

"One sister," he said.

"And who's been the chieftain while you were gone?"

"My mother has been filling the role. She's currently still chieftess until I take a mate." He grinned. "I guess she isn't anymore, and you are, but we'll get that all squared away when we arrive. It'll take us about half a gemoon in this ship. If you're not already pregnant by then—"

"Wait, what?" I touched my chest. "I have a birth control implant. You wouldn't think that I'd go into the ring like I did capable of getting pregnant?"

"Oh," he said, obviously surprised. He hadn't thought about that at all. "I see."

"Is this a bad thing?" I said. I wasn't sure about his reaction.

"Well, the mating bond will stay at this level of violence until I impregnate you," he said. "And, uh, I… it's not easy for me losing control of my body all the time."

I nodded slowly, taking this in.

"Would you consider removing the implant?"

"Uh… right now?"

"You said it when we were talking about this, before you accepted the bond. You knew this meant having my young."

"I…" I nodded. But words were getting stuck in my throat.

"You want that, don't you?"

"I do." I wanted a family. I wanted to be a mother and to feel that bond with children, to matter so deeply to a little being's life. But... this was fast. "It's just... if we could have a little time to get used to each other first."

He didn't say anything.

"Well, let me think about it," I said, biting down on my lip. "It's kind of a big deal. You want me to go to this new planet, meet your family, become a chieftess, learn a new language, and all of that while my body is trying to support and grow a new life? It's... it's a lot."

"No, it is," he said, and he looked chagrined again. "I'm sorry."

"But... from your perspective, losing control of yourself... I guess that's hard."

"I feel as though I haven't been in control of myself in years," he said. "The Toth have controlled me. And now, this bond... it's not unpleasant, but..." He got up from the table. "All right, let's try something, all right? After we get the ship off this planet and spaceside? Let me try to see if I can be slow with you?"

"You mean, with, um, with sex?" I said.

He nodded. "If I can get some control over the mating madness, it might be all right."

"Okay," I said.

"Amongst my people, the tradition is that once a mating bond has been accepted, the couple goes away on a noccht, which is a long stretch of time for them to be alone in a special place away from the clan, until the woman becomes pregnant. I had thought that we could go and do that when you arrive. But if you can't become pregnant, I don't know what the point of it would be."

"I'm messing with your cultural traditions," I said. "I'm sorry."

"You're not," he said. "You're not doing anything

wrong. We simply hadn't talked about this."

He was right, but I felt bad. "When I was talking to Caspe, he said something about your strands, that you have them because your females don't ovulate unless it's triggered by orgasm."

Hugo rubbed one of his horns, making a thoughtful face. "It's been a while since I've had a biology class, but I think I understand that. Don't humans function that way?"

"We ovulate on a cycle, once a month, regardless of sexual activity," I said. "It's likely easier for you to impregnate a woman of your species, because she probably releases an egg because of having sex, and with humans, you have to time it right. There are only a few fertile days a every cycle."

"Oh," he said, continuing to rub his horn. "And how long are the cycles?"

"Twenty-eight Earth sun-cycles give or take," I said.

"So, it could take us quite some time, even if you remove the implant. I really think you should." He made a face. "But maybe I'm being selfish, just not wanting the mating madness. Let's experiment. If I can control it, I can give you more time. And I want to be able to do that."

TWELVE

rowan

We finished breakfast. I finished posting my debt payments. Hugo sent messages to his family. And then we buckled in and got on the shipcomms with the tower and got permission to leave the dock and got into the takeoff queue.

After we blasted off and we finally got out into the upper atmosphere, we made the jump into deep space, and then we unbuckled our seatbelts and looked at each other.

Hugo took me to his quarters. We hadn't shared a bed last night, and I decided not to ask about it, because of being so exhausted. For all I knew, in his culture, mates didn't share a bed. Their mating activities seemed sort of athletic, so maybe it wasn't typically associated with night time. Also, I got the impression their mating was much more focused on, uh, mating—making babies—than a pleasure activity like humans were.

Well, and the Toth also, to be honest.

Of course, it obviously *was* pleasurable for him. I should ask, but I didn't want to offend him again with all my questions, in case I sounded disparaging. I worried a little, though. He said that the violence of the bond would disappear when I was pregnant. Would he not want to have sex at all after I was knocked up?

I'd never been pregnant, but I didn't think I was going to lose all interest in sex when I was.

We stood looking down on the sleeping berth in his quarters, which honestly wasn't really big enough for two people to stretch out on, but I thought we could fit if we snuggled. I wanted to sleep in the same bed as him, and I would have to ask him to try it, at least, at some point.

But this was all going to be an exercise in give and take, each of us needing to be sensitive to the other's compromises. I couldn't ask him to make all of them. On the other hand, I was the one going into the complete unknown, so that did tend to mean that I was at a disadvantage compared to him.

"So," he said softly, "if, um, you weren't mated to a man, what would you usually do to, uh, start things?"

I shrugged. "Kiss?"

"Yeah?" He looked cheered by this. "Okay, that's pretty similar with me, uh, with my people."

"Do you… do you have sex if you're not mated?"

"Oh, sure," he said. "Definitely. You can't figure out if you're mated unless you have sex, so you definitely have sex with people who don't end up being your mates. Otherwise, what, I would have been a virgin?"

"Right," I said, shaking my head. "You're obviously not."

"No, trust me, every eligible woman in my clan tried to get my mating bond to trigger for them."

"Every woman? We're going back to your clan, and they've all boned you?"

He gave me a mischievous grin. "Jealous?"

"How many women are we talking about? How big is your clan?"

He reached out and caressed my cheek. "Remember the several times I've explained that I've never felt anything like what I feel with you?"

I had to smile at that. "Yeah."

"There is no comparison when it comes to my mate." His voice went growly. "You have no reason to be jealous."

I kissed him.

Our tongues danced, and I moaned against his mouth and—

He pulled away and threw himself against the opposite wall, panting.

Right. He was trying to control his madness rising. I decided it was better to be quiet, and I just waited until he could look at me again.

"Okay," he whispered, his voice still raspy. "First kissing, and then what?"

"I..." I felt shy. I blushed and looked at my feet.

"What I'd like to do is start with your breasts," he said softly. "I'd like to uncover them and fondle them and then lick them—"

"That sounds good." I met his gaze, my own voice going throaty as well. "Perfect, in fact."

He let out a grunt and shut his eyes.

Another prolonged pause until he managed to get his breathing under control. "Then what?"

"If talking about it is making it hard for you to stay in control, then I don't see how doing it—"

"I know," he said. "But let's just see how long I can keep pushing it down, okay?"

I nodded. "Well, I guess typically, I'd need a lot of foreplay. Kissing, touching me all over, and then... after I'm wet, then, my, um, then my..." I looked away and whispered it. "My pussy."

"I want to lick you there," he said in a very gravelly voice.

My body twitched. "Please?"

"You wouldn't mind?"

"Mind? Are you kidding?"

"The scent of you there. I can't imagine how much better it would be to taste you."

I bit down on my lip, thinking of his flat, dark tongue between the lips of me, against my clit, and I shuddered.

Suddenly, I was on my back on his sleeping berth and he was on top of me.

I gasped. "You lost your fight with the madness?"

"I'm fighting it," he grunted.

"I see that," I said. "Sort of."

"I'm going to keep my clothes on," he said. "Let's just take off yours." He was working at my pants.

I helped him.

He yanked them down around my hips, down to my knees and he put his face to my pelvis and breathed me in.

I don't know why him smelling me was so hot, but it *was*. I threw back my head, a thrill going through me.

He kissed me, his mouth against my mound, and then moved lower to kiss over my sensitive lips. His tongue ran over the seam of me. Once. Twice. Three times.

And I parted for him.

He let out a deeply satisfied noise. "You taste…"

I moaned, trying to spread my legs for him, but my pants were still around my knees, and I couldn't really open for him.

His tongue delved into me, soft, textured, wondrous. Everything started to tingle.

"You taste perfect," he breathed. "Better than I thought you would."

I moaned again, pressing up into him, my pelvis against his face.

He eagerly licked me in response.

I reached down to touch him and found his horns. Were they made precisely for me to hold onto while he licked me like this? Because I thought they might be.

I wrapped my hands around each one and tugged his face close.

He made an approving grunt and licked again. He swirled around my opening, and that felt good and I hummed a bit. And then he moved higher until he found my clit, and I made a much louder noise, and he chuckled against me and stayed there for some time, only occasionally returning to my opening before going back to lick textured patterns against my most sensitive area.

It was phenomenal, and I quickly lost all sense of time, and then all sense of space, and then all sense of anything except the rhythmic lap of him against me.

I might have made noises—they might have been embarrassing—I might have moved. I was pretty sure my pelvis was doing spastic things occasionally, not in any rhythm either, just… because… because I was *lost*.

He brought me to the edge of an orgasm—riding some height of bright lights and streaming movement—and then stopped abruptly, throwing his head back, gritting his teeth, eyes squeezed shut.

I looked up at him, still holding his horns. I was out of breath and disoriented. "What? Why did you…?"

"Fighting it," he managed.

I let go of his horns.

His neck corded.

I tensed.

And then, above me, he convulsed. He was on me like a wild thing unleashed, and it was even more intense than it had been any other time, and I wondered if it had been because he was trying to keep it back for so long. His mouth went to my neck, and I felt his teeth scrape me there.

He pulled back his head and then drove it at me, one of his horns catching in the soft flesh of my arm.

I cried out at the bright spot of pain.

But his strands were locking on now, and my clit felt one bit of vibration and immediately convulsed into a little climax, because I had been so sensitized already by his tongue. I was wet this time, and when his cock entered me, it didn't hurt, even though he ripped into me the way he always did, just forcing his thickness inside and stretching me full of his girth and throbbing hardness.

I felt him in my body, and now that the strands were locked on, I could feel his pleasure too, could feel how warm and wet and slick I was to his sensitive cock, how good the walls of me stroked him.

I didn't care about the pain. This was amazing. I kissed him.

He took my bottom lip between his teeth.

I let out a sob-cry.

His cock was thrusting, and it was good, and I was moving with him, and his strands pulsed into me in time with his movement.

I came.

The orgasm was a hot rush of intensity, almost painful because it was so much and because it took me over with no warning.

He slammed himself into me and came too, letting

out some garbled noise, and I felt the echo of it through his strands, through our bond, and I felt it was half-painful for him too, how it had tipped over due to his feeling my pleasure.

I wheezed.

He was rigid over me, also breathing hard.

When he did speak, it was in his own language, those words I was taking to be expletives. I had heard him say them before.

I petted him, trying to calm my breathing, rubbing the fur on his neck, where it disappeared into the shirt he was wearing. We were neither of us completely undressed, but I had managed to part my legs, so…

Yup, more of my clothes were ripped. That was kind of becoming a liability. I wondered if I should really bother getting dressed while we were on this ship?

He lowered his face to my shoulder. "You're bleeding."

"Am I?" Oh, it was my arm. I looked down at the bright spot of blood seeping into my shirt. Now it hurt again.

"I'm sorry."

"You didn't mean it," I said.

"I held the madness off, but then—"

"It was twice as intense," I said.

"Your orgasm was so much, I felt it like—" He lifted his head again.

"Yeah," I said.

He looked down at me. "This is… so good and so not good all at the same time."

I shook my head. "It's all good. Nothing about it is not good."

He laughed helplessly. "Roots and branches," he muttered.

"Kiss me," I ordered.

He did.

Whatever this was, it felt *right*, and that was all I particularly cared about at the moment.

THIRTEEN

I couldn't believe I hadn't thought about her birth control. It only made sense, after all, but it honestly hadn't occurred to me, and now I felt like a gratts for asking her to remove it. She wasn't wrong that this was all going to be a lot for her, so much change at once, and to ask her to do that while she was also pregnant… how could I do that?

But how could I do anything when my mating madness triggered every time I was around her? Truthfully, I could hardly predict it. It didn't seem to happen every time I got aroused. I could be a little hard and not have it riding up my spine, but then, once it started, it was next to impossible to hold it down forever.

It was probably a miracle I'd been able to lick her pussy as long as I had. That had been divine. I wanted to do that again. I wanted to do it right, starting with her breasts as I'd said. I wanted to lick her all over.

We rested together in my sleeping berth, falling into a light nap with our bodies entwined.

I woke up to her mouth on mine, and I wanted her again.

She had taken everything off at some point, and I could feel her smooth, warm body wriggling against me.

I yanked my shirt off so that our bare skin could touch and I put my mouth to her pretty breasts. I kissed the slopes of them and the little dusky circles surrounding her nipples. I kissed the nipples until they puckered.

She sighed, eyes closed, one hand in my fur, one hand on one of my horns.

This made me remember that I'd wounded her arm.

I moved over to examine it.

"Hugo," she whimpered. "Why did you stop?"

"Mmm, just a hisec, pretty Rowan." I licked away the dried blood on her wound.

She gasped at that too.

"You'll be all right," I told her, kissing her scab. "I'm so sorry."

"It's okay," she said to me. "Back to what you were doing?"

I laughed a little, tongue going to run over her breasts.

She moaned, pleased.

"I'm thinking of a different strategy," I said.

"Strategy?"

"We try to tire out the madness," I said. "If I fuck you over and over again, eventually, I'll completely empty out my balls and I'll be able to control myself."

"Okay," she breathed, tugging on my horn, pulling my mouth back to her breast. "Good idea."

"I thought so too," I said, rolling over top of her.

But we were naked, skin on skin, and my strands took this opportunity to lock on. Now, hooked in place, there was no way I was getting my tongue back on her delicious pussy, and this disappointed me.

"Mmm, I want your cock again, Hugo," she

murmured. "I can feel you hard and ready through the bond, and I want you to put it back in me."

"Is that what I should do with my cock?" I teased her, voice frayed.

"Yes, it belongs inside me. Put it back," she whispered. "Please."

* * *

hugo

I fucked her all morning. We fucked, slept, woke up, fucked again, stumbled out naked to eat food, fucked on the table, finished eating, fucked in the corridor back to my bedchamber, and then I bent her over the sleeping berth and spread her legs and pounded her like that too.

One of my strands locked on just underneath the pucker of her asshole, which she liked, and I could feel that through the bond. I think that surprised both of us.

She had handfuls of the bedsheets, crying out little noises that made me harder and more turned on, and neither of us lasted any time at all before we exploded together, like a rain of hot, glowing sparks.

Then she pulled me down with her and we kissed sleepily and I held her in my arms.

She was sore now. I'd felt it when I'd been inside her, and no matter how much the strands forced her to accommodate me, it wasn't sustainable. Worse, it wasn't working. There seemed to be no flagging in my sexual appetite or capability. Maybe being mated was doing that, putting me in some heightened physical state.

But if so, and our conversation about the physical differences of our species was true, then my body was designed for a quick burst of intense sexual activity until I managed to successfully breed a female. This, with Rowan, it wasn't going to go that way, and it might take a physical toll on me.

But I should stop feeling sorry for myself and accept that it wasn't anything like growing young in my own body. If I got her pregnant, her physical toll would be much more intense. Furthermore, simply accommodating my large member was taking a physical toll on her. She was small and soft and vulnerable, and I needed to be careful with her.

"Do mates share a bed in your culture?" she whispered into my chest. She was absently playing with the stubble under my pecks, body fur the Toth had forced me to shave.

"During mating, yes," I said, looking affectionately down at her. "Sometimes beyond that, also, but young like to sleep with their mothers, especially when they are nursing, so sometimes that becomes crowded and the male is the least necessary to that dynamic, so he's the first to go."

She grinned up at me. "Oh, well, I guess I see that."

"We are warm-blooded creatures like any other," I said. "We love the warmth and closeness of each other."

"Well, except the Toth," she said.

It was true. The Toth were renowned for their lack of affection with each other, their standoffishness. Maybe that was why they were so violent a species, because they didn't get enough snuggling.

"So, we will sleep together?"

"As long as you wish it," I said, running my hand down her small, smooth back.

She cuddled into me. "I wish it. I can't imagine not wishing it. I know we've only known each other a short time, but I want to be near you all the time. I never want to let go of you."

I felt this too. I crushed her close, kissing her, and she wrapped her thighs around me as if trying to get us even closer.

I grunted, feeling the mating instinct trying to rise again. I separated us.

She let out a cry of disappointment. "Hugo—"

"You need a rest. Your body needs to heal from everything I've put it through." I didn't say out loud that we'd also done it for no reason at all since she couldn't get pregnant.

"It's fine," she muttered throatily. "I don't mind being a little sore."

I knew this was true. She was eager for me, and her body was so responsive to me. I kissed her again, slower, softer. "We should sleep," I said.

* * *

rowan

Hugo and I had our first honest-to-stars fight the next morning when I woke up to him examining my body, and I had a few bruises.

I felt… well, my whole body felt used and a little sore, muscles I hadn't used in a while getting a real workout, and my sensitive places throbbing and swollen in a way that wasn't the least bit unpleasant. It was like the way a person usually feels in the beginning of a relationship, when you end up having lots of sex naturally anyway, even without a mating bond, but several times more intense.

Similarly, I was so attuned to Hugo. His voice— either in Cobran or when he put on the modifier to speak in Common—was familiar to me, and I loved the deep, affectionate tones of it, the way it softened when he spoke to me, how he grunted and groaned when he was inside me. When the strands were connected, I could feel him, and I loved that. It made sex so much more intimate, feeling him in that way, knowing he felt me too.

I was falling in love with him.

It had only been a day of bouts of sex, maybe, but peppered with little conversations, asking each other about our respective cultures, our families, telling little stories here and there about our childhoods, all those little things that bring two people closer.

I'd almost said it while we were fucking. It had been on the tip of my tongue, and I'd swallowed it, because it was too soon, even if we were mated.

And then, we were fighting.

He was yelling, but I could tell he wasn't angry at me, but at himself for having hurt me.

And I was mad because he wasn't respecting my ability to make choices about my body.

"No sex today," he said.

"You don't get to say that," I countered.

Soon, our voices were rising and then I swept out of his quarters wrapped in a blanket, snapping the door closed on him as I stalked away from him.

I realized this was dumb. My side of the argument had been that we should definitely engage in more fucking, and we couldn't fuck if we weren't in the same room.

I kept walking, though, unwilling to break. Then I stopped, thought about it, and then I turned around and went back for his room.

But he was coming for me.

"I'm sorry," he said, just as I said it at the same time.

And then we kissed.

He pulled me into his massive, hard chest, which

was bare. He was only wearing a pair of pants. He rubbed my back.

I held onto him, which meant that I lost hold on the blanket, and then I wasn't wearing anything.

He broke the kiss, eyes darkening as he looked down at my breasts. Then, his gaze snagged on a bruise on my skin, and he stiffened, gently running his thumb over it.

"It looks worse than it is," I said. "I've always bruised easily. I have pale skin, so you can see it easier."

He shook his head. "Rowan, when the strands are attached, I can feel how hurt you are."

"I'm a little sore, but it's not bad," I said.

"I don't want you sore," he said. "I don't want to hurt you."

"I know," I said. "You're not doing it on purpose, but the mating madness just makes you a little crazy. And it's hot, you know, and everything about the way you fuck me is really, really good."

"I thought if I could tire myself out, it would help me have more control, but it didn't work," he said. "So, I don't seem to be able to hold it off, and I can't wear myself out. I don't have any other ideas yet, but we need to figure this out."

"Well, I could have you in my mouth again," I said.

He let out a sharp breath. "That was... was that really all right for you?"

I smiled. "Yes, I liked it. A lot."

"Maybe, for today, I can try to just touch myself and use your mouth a few times while we think about what to try."

Why did his saying he was going to 'use' my mouth make me so hot?

"I… I didn't mean to, um, say—" He cringed. "I would never *use* you—"

"Use me, Hugo. Use my mouth now." I slid down to my knees to unfasten his fly and take him out.

He panted down at me, and I watched his cock lengthen and thicken. "You like being used, Rowan?" His voice was a rasp.

I took his hardness in both hands and stroked it. "I like everything about this big, pretty cock. If it needs to come, I want to help it. Is that what you need, Hugo?"

He shuddered. "Rowan, sometimes… the things you…"

I licked the dark, gleaming head of him.

He pushed between my lips.

I moaned, urging him on, sucking on him.

He rocked deeper into my mouth, and his strands did their thing. "You liked it when people watched us," he rasped.

I made a noise of protest. Not this again.

But he was in my mouth, and his strands were locked in, holding us together. I wasn't going to be able to talk.

The strands sent their clever little lines of tingling pleasure through my body. My nipples tightened and throbbed, and my clit swelled.

I groaned as the head of his cock invaded my mouth, as the strands altered me to take him here. It turned me on, I had to admit. Something about the very act itself, my submissive posture, using my mouth for his pleasure, all of it was heady and thrilling.

He was looking down at me, something in his gaze, something I hadn't quite seen before, a hard glitter in his eyes.

It made me hotter. My core clenched.

I clamped my legs tightly closed, squeezing my sensitive places. I'd had so many orgasms lately that everything down there was even more sensitive than usual anyway. I was primed.

"Used," he breathed, his voice insubstantial. "Watched."

I moaned around his cock.

He pushed it down my throat.

"Taken," he growled. "Claimed. And you like it."

I moaned harder, and now I started to grind my hips, just sort of using the pressure of my legs there and the slight bit of movement I manage to ride against the pleasure his strands gave me. It was enough, more than enough. I was shot into a dark, sweet, dirty place of pleasure right away.

He felt it through the strands.

I felt him feel it, and felt his cock get harder. He shut his eyes and then opened them, and when he did, he was in that sweet, dirty place too.

I held his gaze, sucking him, grinding my hips, loving it.

"Raise your hands above your head," he panted.

I obeyed without thinking.

He snatched them up with one hand and pinned them to the wall, which pushed my back into the wall, and now I was plastered there, and his body was in front of me, and he was invading my mouth, and it was even hotter, even better.

"What kind of girl *are* you, Rowan?" he ground out, fucking my mouth in jerking motions.

I couldn't answer, but I made noise around his cock. I massaged him with my tongue. He felt good in there. My whole body was throbbing. There were sparks traveling down to my nipples, bouncing against my clit, and then heading back up to the sensitive parts of my tongue. In addition to all of that, I was getting his pleasure through the strands, feeling how hard and needy his cock was.

He wanted to come, but he couldn't.

I had to come first. I had to release him.

Remembering this almost sent me over the edge, but I stopped it, releasing my thighs, giving myself a little breather to let off the pressure. We were playing a little game together now.

He had me trapped, but he was mine, and his pleasure belonged to me.

"Are you a *filthy* sort of girl?"

I groaned, clamping my legs back together.

We both felt the jolt of my pleasure at the sensation.

His cock slammed into the back of my throat and he cried out.

"Are you a filthy *slut?*"

I crested, a half-orgasm. My whole body trembled.

"*My* filthy slut," he decided, his body spasming too, his orgasm just out of his reach. "You *belong* to me."

I made some sort of noise, something muffled by his cock in my mouth but keening, and I came so hard that I was afraid I was going to bite him, and I felt myself jerking against him where he was holding my wrists against the wall.

The pleasure was a white-hot supernova. It took away everything—my sense of smell and taste and sight—and replaced it all with the most intense pleasure I thought I'd ever felt.

So, I didn't notice that Hugo had let go of me, or that he was pulling the strands out of my face, trying to disengage from me, not until the tail end of the little earthquakes were racking my body, and that's when I realized he looked… upset.

He tucked his still-hard dick away and fastened his pants. He looked at me and then looked away.

"Hugo?" I whispered. I wiped at my lips. I could taste his skin, but none of his ejaculate, because he'd been too far down my throat when he came.

His hands were shaking. "Sorry," he said. "I'm sorry. I would never call you… I don't know why I…" He backed up.

I stood up. "It's okay," I said gently. "That was really good. That was really intense. You felt how much I liked that."

"I did," he breathed, but this didn't seem to be a particularly good thing. "I definitely did." He ran a hand over his face, tugging on one of his horns. "Let's just take the day. We both need a *break*." And then he turned and stalked away from me without saying anything else, without waiting for a response from me.

FOURTEEN

hugo

I decided not to think about what had happened with us, what I'd done to her, what I'd said to her, how much I'd liked it, none of it.

I didn't know how to think about it.

I only knew that something about it was unbearable, and that I couldn't engage with it.

I avoided her for the rest of the day, even though I could see it hurt her. She came to find me once and she was quiet and unsure. She stood in the doorway, twisting her fingers together, and she looked small and vulnerable, and I thought about the savage way I kept fucking her and it made my stomach turn over.

I told her I was tired and that it had nothing to do with her.

I knew she didn't believe it. She tried to bring it up, but I shut her down.

I said we should sleep alone that night, and I thought she might start crying, but she didn't do it in front of me, if she did. She ran off and I didn't see her again.

Not until I woke up screaming in the middle of the night, and she was coming through the door with a plastorch, her voice soothing as she knelt next to my bed and put her hand on my chest. "You're dreaming. You're dreaming."

I seized her, pulling her down onto my sleeping berth, kissing her anywhere I could get my mouth. "It's the arena. I have them sometimes, always about fights."

She soothed me, hands everywhere. "Of course you do. You're safe now. You never have to go back."

I crushed her against me. I was shaking.

"You're with me, Hugo. You're safe."

Our lips met, and then our tongues.

And then we made love, and it was slow and soft for the first time. I didn't know why the bond let it happen. Maybe my body was too frightened for more violence. I didn't know, but I was glad to let it happen in increments, glad to take the time to kiss her everywhere I wanted, glad that when I finally penetrated her, she was slick with her own arousal, and that we could just slowly rock against each other as our tongues stroked each other in the same time to our slow, rhythmic joining.

Her orgasm came through the bond like a slow flow of thick, sweet liquid. It surrounded us both until it filled us up and rocked us into bursting.

After, she clung to me. "Let's not fight again."

I stroked her hair. "We weren't fighting."

"You don't have to be rough with me if it doesn't turn you on."

"Let's not talk about that."

"But Hugo—"

"I'm falling in love with you, Rowan Llox, let's just… *please*."

She gasped, lifting her head, searching my gaze.

I winced. Had I said that out loud?

"Me too." She nodded. "I'm falling in love with you too."

I kissed her.

She burrowed into me.

After that, it was different.

The rest of the trip was easier. We slept in the bed every night, and we fucked in the morning and in the evening, but rarely more than that. I could have. I wanted to. I thought she wanted to as well. But I thought of those bruises on her skin, or the way I'd felt her surge of pleasure after I called her names, and…

The madness rose, but I controlled it enough to get away and masturbate in the showers and not touch her beyond twice a day.

If she tried to talk about it, I changed the subject.

And we started saying it, that we loved each other. We said it when we were making love and when we were eating, and when we were working on teaching her my language.

I had nightmares every night.

I was likely just getting the arena out of my system.

Once we got to Abbunia, everything was going to be better.

I was sure of it.

FIFTEEN

rowan

Hugo and I came out of deep space to a flurry of messages from his mother, which he went through on his own, looking down at a screen on the ship.

"What?" I said nervously in Treebark people language, which was called Rrolln. "What does she say?"

Hugo absently corrected my pronunciation, still staring at the screen. He drew his shaggy brows together. The hair on his chest had been growing over the past half gemoon. He was hairy all over, and I liked it.

I got up and went over to where he was sitting. "Hugo," I said in Common.

He pulled me down on his lap. "It's mostly about real estate developers trying to buy our forest to build a resort for offworlders to come and vacation."

"Oh," I said. "Your mother would never sell." The trees were sacred to Hugo's people. He didn't personally believe the trees had souls, he said, but some of his people did, and he respected their beliefs and venerated them. There were other reasons to protect trees anyway, like the benefit for the ecosystem of Abbunia.

"No," he said, "but they're persistent." He kissed my

neck, nuzzling me under my ear.

That felt good, and I snuggled into him. "She has to have said something about the fact you have a human mate."

"Very little, actually."

I turned to look at him, worried. "Is that bad?"

"Don't know," he said.

"Be straight with me, Hugo," I said. "Is your mother going to hate me?"

"No," he said. "She will love you, because you are imminently lovable."

"I think you're biased," I said. "Because we have orgasms together."

He chuckled.

Truth be told, I wasn't sure how he felt about me. He had started saying that he loved me, and we said it all the time now. He behaved in a loving way toward me. He was good to me. But... I don't know... I worried that he might be in love with only a certain version of me, and that I might be too flawed for him to really love.

It wasn't as if anyone ever had loved me, anyway.

People didn't notice me. My parents never paid me much mind. My mom... well, all I ever said to anyone about my mom was that she was dead, and that she'd died when I was too young to remember. My dad had fed me, but otherwise mostly ignored me.

Maybe I was being silly about it, but Hugo did tend to spend time away from me every day on the ship. I don't know what I had expected, because if we'd spent every waking hidosec together, we probably would have been at each other's throats. It was healthy to spend time apart.

But maybe he was just bored with me already or

something.

I knew he sometimes masturbated instead of having sex with me. Which, well, I was doing that, too, because being around him, I was aroused basically constantly. I would have preferred for us to be having sex, though. I guessed not so much for Hugo?

It wasn't as if we weren't having sex. We still did, two or three times every day, which—in any other relationship—I would have thought was plenty, even a bit excessive, but we were mated and I was hot for him all the time.

I told myself that he was probably just weirded out about bruising me, because I knew he'd gotten concerned after that, and I also noticed there had been no blow jobs since that hot and heavy session in the corridor. It would be better if he was concerned about me, not, um, disinterested.

I couldn't quite make myself believe it, though.

No one ever found me interesting. I had been invisible my whole life.

Even now, he wasn't paying attention to me.

Yes, Rowan, he's checking his messages from home. He's a chieftain, for stars sake. You can't be threatened by him doing his job.

I wouldn't be.

"Oh, curse my mother," he said with a groan.

"What?" I gave him an expectant look, and I had switched to Rrolln. I needed to speak as much as I could in it.

"I just sent her a quick message to say that we were in orbit," he said, in Cobran. "And she said that she's going to gather the entire clan to come and meet us when we dock."

"That's not bad." I said it in Rrolln.

He gave me a little smile and corrected my pronunciation. "Just talk in Cobran, love."

"I want to do it in Rrolln, though."

"You don't have to."

I switched to Cobran, defeated. "Just tell me how not to disappoint the clan. What should I wear? What should I say?"

He grinned at me. "You're amazing."

"I'm not," I said. "I want to be a good chieftess for your people." *I want them to like me.* "But... should I do the thing you taught me, the greeting?" I touched my forehead and lowered my hand, palm up, bowing my head.

"Uh, no, that's just for members of the chieftain's family. The people will do that to you."

"Oh," I said. "And I should do it to your mother. And sister."

"Yes." He nodded.

"I should come up with something to say, though. A greeting? Will you help me fix my pronunciation if I get it wrong? I don't want to offend anyone."

"This is what I'm saying though. You're all stressed out, and my mother isn't being the least bit considerate, and—"

"It's fine." I shook my head. "It'll just be something short and sweet. It's no bother at all, unless it's a bother for you to help with my pronunciation, in which case, don't worry about it. I'll figure it out on my own with the phrasebook we found in the ship's library." I scampered up off his lap. "In fact, just don't worry about anything. I'll do it all myself."

"Are you sure?" He was grinning at me, affection all over him.

I nodded. "Definitely. I don't want to be a bother to

you. I'm sure you have so much else to worry about right now."

"You're never a bother." His voice got a little growly. He reached for me and pulled me back onto his lap. He kissed me hard.

My body woke up at that. I squirmed into him. "Maybe there are other things we should do instead?"

He panted. "No. No, you should, uh, leave me alone for a bit."

Right. I forced myself to smile. "Okay." I got up again.

"I love you," he said, looking up at me.

"I love you, too," I said. Then I left to go digging through my clothes and try to find something appropriate for meeting an entire clan. I ended up deciding on a dress. Nothing too fancy. It was dark blue and it was made of a soft, comfortable material. It hung on my curves without clinging too obscenely, and it was flattering. I figured it could look casual or dressy depending on the accessories, but I didn't dress it up too much, not going for any jewelry. I also didn't spend a lot of time with my hair. This was both because I didn't think that putting hair up was a particularly great way to ingratiate myself to this group of hairy people, and because I wanted to spend time on crafting my little greeting.

When the ship docked, I was going over it for the third time, double checking my pronunciation as best I could.

Hugo came looking for me, and when he saw me, his eyes got cloudy. "You look, um…" His gaze swept me and he swallowed. "Beautiful." His voice dropped into a lower register.

I felt shy and pleased.

"Roots and branches, how am I going to control myself?" He groaned.

"We could… do we have time…?"

He wavered in the doorway, looking at me, and I could see him considering it. Suddenly, he lurched across the room, wrapping an arm around me.

We kissed.

"Just lift your skirt and take you against this wall?" he rasped.

"Yes," I breathed, shivering.

"Fuck, Rowan," he grunted. "I want you."

"Take me," I said, eager. "Take me, Hugo, *now*."

So, he did.

After, he breathed apologies in my ear, and I told him not to be sorry in a throaty voice. He had *nothing* to be sorry about.

"I hurt you. You weren't wet."

"The strands made it fine," I assured him. "I'm not hurt." So, maybe it *was* about this. We were going to need to talk about it.

"I messed up your hair," he said.

I ran my fingers through it, blushing. "Will your people think I look too untidy?"

"No, but they're going to be able to smell that we were, uh…"

"Oh." I flushed harder.

He kissed me. "You *are* my mate. It's all right."

"I should find a comb."

"I shouldn't have done it."

"*We* did it," I said. "Together. It wasn't just you. And I love you, and I love your cock, and I love your cock in me, so… we should have." I grinned at him.

He kissed me again. "You're perfect," he said. "Everything about you is perfection."

My smile wavered. I did *not* believe him.

He put his arm around me, settling it on my hip, his massive palm resting comfortably there.

That felt nice. Next to him, I felt small and engulfed, and I looked up at him and I had a wave of emotion. I was so lucky to have found him. He had bonded to me, even though we were so different. He'd let me become his mate and his chieftess, and I was in love with him.

Stop looking for things to worry about and try to just be happy, Rowan, I scolded myself.

He kissed my forehead. "Let's get this over with."

"Come on, aren't you happy to be home?" I said, smiling up at him.

"Of course I am," he said. "But I wanted to ease you into this."

"Don't worry about me," I told him. "Please?"

"It's my job to worry about you. I have to protect you."

"Not from your people, especially if they're going to be my people too."

He studied my expression. "You really are amazing, Rowan."

"Stop saying stuff like that." I bounced on the heels of my feet. "Let's go."

So, we did. We went through the ship, and out the door onto the exit ramp.

Outside, we were greeted by cool, muggy air. It was just cool enough that I might have liked a sweater or small jacket, but I had Hugo, so I snuggled into his warmth.

Immediately, there was a sound, a loud yipping, and I looked out to see that a sea of people like Hugo were all standing in front of the ship, all with their heads thrown back, letting out the noise.

Some were holding onto their horns, and some had stretched their hands toward the sky.

I eyed them with interest, wanting to see how they differed from Hugo, the only one of his kind I'd ever seen. The men seemed to be of a similar height to Hugo, though several were taller than him and some had horns that were thicker. The women were smaller, with thin and delicate horns that curved coyly around their faces. Many of them seemed to have decorated them with shimmering patterns that had been painted. The women were beautiful and graceful and I felt odd and awkward.

I snuggled closer to Hugo.

He tightened his grip on me.

When we reached the bottom of the exit ramp, the yips quieted, and all of the clan touched their foreheads and lowered their palms, bowing their heads at us.

Hugo lifted his hand and motioned for them to raise their gazes. He spoke in Rrolln. "Thank you for this fine welcome, and I am glad to be home. I present to you my mate, Rowan."

At least I was pretty sure that was what he said. There were some words I kept getting confused. I thought he had attempted to use words that I knew, though, for my benefit.

I smiled out at the people. "It is my honor to be here on Abbunia. I look forward to coming to know you all and living among you. I am humbled and blessed to have mated with your chieftain, and I hope to be able to be worthy of both him and you all."

The people yipped again.

Hugo grinned at me. "Your pronunciation was perfect," he whispered in my ear in Common.

I beamed.

One of the Treebark people came forward and took me by the arm, pulling me out into the throng of the crowd of the clan.

Hugo reached for me in alarm. "Wait!"

The Treebark person did the royal greeting to me again. "Welcome, Chieftess Rowan," he said. Then he lifted his hand, tilting it so that his fingertips were at an angle.

Hugo was there, speaking rapidly in Rrolln to the man, and I couldn't keep up.

The Treeperson spoke back, shaking his head and gesturing.

I looked back and forth between them and then out at the gathered throng of people, all of whom were looking at me. I couldn't deny that was kind of nifty. I didn't mind that at all, as long as I didn't do anything to screw up too much.

I raised my hand to mimic what the Treeperson had done.

Another Treeperson, this one a woman, also speaking rapid Rrolln, put her fingertips against mine and then she said, "Hello."

"Hello?" I said, grinning at her. I felt an excitement swelling inside me.

I turned to another Treeperson and touched fingertips with him. "Hello?"

"Hello!" he said, smiling widely. He punctuated this with some yipping and some laughter.

I was delighted. I began weaving my way amongst the people, saying hello to each of them and putting my fingertips against theirs. I was happy and they were happy. They touched my face and my hair, curious. We yipped at each other.

A baby Treeperson was thrust into my arms. He had

tiny little horn nubs, and I'd never seen something quite so cute.

Hugo caught up to me, putting his arm around me. He spoke in my ear, in Common. "I'm sorry. You don't have to do this."

"Don't make me stop?" I pleaded. I was still holding the baby. "Will our babies look like this?"

He pressed his lips to my temple.

I handed the baby back to his mother and pressed my fingertips against the next person of the clan, crowing, "Hello!"

"Hello, Chieftess!" they cried back at me.

It became a chant. They clapped and touched their foreheads and stomped their feet, and I twirled in Hugo's arms, and I think it was the best day of my life.

I'd never felt so… seen.

SIXTEEN

hugo

"Wasn't she amazing?" I was in my mother's office, which looked out over the Stran Lagoon, blue-green tree fronds leaning over the water, floating on the surface. I had forgotten how beautiful it was in Abbunia. I couldn't stop staring at the trees and the sky. It was odd, but the sight of them hurt me somehow, made my soul feel emotions I didn't know how to understand. "I have to say, I wasn't pleased that you assembled everyone to meet us, but she rose to the occasion with aplomb. And the people love her."

"Yes, it does seem so." My mother's voice was sour.

My shoulders slumped. "You did it on purpose. You wanted to overwhelm her."

"That seems a horribly petty and cruel thing to do."

I rounded on her. "Mother."

"Mating isn't everything, son. And you said she wasn't with child, so? If she goes back home, your bond will break within the moon-cycle and you'll be free to mate with someone else."

"With who? I've attempted with every eligible female in the clan." I shook my head at her. "You really want me to send Rowan away?"

"I can't believe you brought her here. You want to put human blood into our bloodline. Those Toths turned you into them, didn't they?"

I drew back, horrified. "Take that back."

"What's next? Perhaps we'll sell off a stretch of the forest so you can have money to become a handler yourself."

"Mother!" I was disgusted. "That's an abominable thing to say."

She glared at me. "It's an abominable thing to do."

"I didn't mean to mate to her. It just happened."

"Oh, I see. Your penis accidentally became stuck inside her. Your strands accidentally locked on?"

"Mother." I winced. I did not want to talk about my penis like that with her.

"How did you mate with a human? You chose her as a pleasure thing as the Toth do?"

My lips parted. "No, it was… part of the fight. They force us to fight over a prize and then we have to…" I grimaced. "I don't want to talk about it." It was reminding me, however, that my mother was a little old fashioned about mating and sex. There was a contingent of people in my clan, mostly older religious people, who had an idea that sex should only be for the creation of children and that there was no other reason for engaging in it at all.

If a man's mating instinct didn't rise for a woman, for instance, he shouldn't have sex with her.

This was stupid, in my opinion, because the mating bond wasn't even necessary for procreation. It definitely made it more likely to happen, but people who didn't mate could still have children.

I'd gone a few rounds with mother about it back when I was coming home from vacations at the university, but it wasn't something I'd given a lot of thought to, lately, especially because my mother had been so insistent that I try to have sex with every woman in the clan to try to get me mated already. Many of them, my mating instinct hadn't even triggered, so I guess I'd thought maybe she'd given up on her ideas, but clearly she hadn't. She'd just been desperate to get me to mate.

Women did not become pregnant from a single sexual encounter, which I thought was to do with whatever Rowan had said to me on the ship, that my people's female's ovulation was triggered by orgasm. I was a little foggy on all the specifics, but I was fairly sure that there was more to it, actually, because I knew that women couldn't trigger ovulation on their own, just from masturbation or something. There had to be semen present for ovulation to happen.

So, the first encounter between two people never resulted in pregnancy, only the second or third after a male's seed was already present in a woman's womb. This meant that my mother hadn't been too worried that I'd leave a string of bastards in the bellies of these women she made me have sex with. She hoped I'd mate with one of them.

While it was tolerated for people to have relationships without a mate, it was very atypical for a chieftain not to have a mating bond, and my mother wanted me mated very much.

I figured she'd just be happy that I was, not that she'd be speciesist about it.

"So, the Toth forced it on you, then. They made you mate to a human."

"The bond rose for her," I said. "She accepted it. You know, it's not the humans' fault the way the Toth treat them. She and her species are victims, just as we are, even more so, since the Toth took so many of them away from their home planet. Now that the wormhole is closed, the humans can never go back home. There is no reason to hate them simply because of their misfortune."

"I have no hatred for humans," she said. "But the Toth have taken enough from our people. They will not take your heir and taint it, forming our people into their image."

"Their image? What are you saying? You know that humans are not Toth. Besides, Mother, let me talk to you a little about dominant genes, shall I? I can assure you, my children with Rowan will more resemble our people than they will take after their human mother."

"Oh, always talking down to me, with your university education. You and your father both. But that education did nothing for us, not when they came for you. I had to give the Toth my only son, and you come back to me and..." She looked me over, and I could see she was distraught. "What have they done to you?"

"I'm fine," I said. "I did what I had to do to protect you and the clan. You have no idea the negotiations that I went through, and if I hadn't been to university, I wouldn't have even known the clauses to look out for, so it *was* worth it."

"You're like them. That's what it did to you. And you want a human girl, just like they do."

"It's not like that," I countered, and I thought about pinning Rowan's hands to the wall and saying she belonged to me. My stomach turned over. I couldn't look at my mother.

"Why did you mate with her?" She came closer, putting a hand on my arm. "Something changed in you, something that made your mating bond rise for her—"

"Stop," I said. I didn't need to hear these words coming out of her mouth, when I'd thought them myself. "It's a biological urge, that's all. It rises for compatible mates, and it rose for her because we'll have strong offspring. It's not about my..." Kinks. "Tastes."

"You admit you prefer human women."

"I prefer *her*," I said. "She's my mate, and we are bonded, and I am only aroused by her, so, in that way, yes, she is my preference. She and I are in love. We have grown very close on the journey here."

"Why isn't she pregnant, then? If you were bonded to her, on a ship with her for half a gemoon, why—"

"She's got an implant."

"A what?"

"It's a medical device that's put into women's skin. It releases hormones that disrupt fertility."

My mother drew back, appalled. "You're mated to a woman who is infertile?"

"No, if she removes the implant—"

"How could the bond rise for her at all?"

"The bond isn't sophisticated enough to discern that sort of thing, Mother. Really, you don't understand—"

"Yes, I'm just so stupid, the woman who bore you and birthed you and raised you." She bared her teeth at me.

I sighed. "I'm sorry."

"Well," said my mother, "why hasn't she removed the implant?"

"We talked about it, but it's her decision," I said. "It's her body. She's left everything she knows, traveled across the galaxy, studied a new language, put up with my..."

"Your what?"

"Their bodies... humans are fragile, and my... urges..." I shook my head. I couldn't find these words. "She's been through enough. I'm not going to ask her to get pregnant immediately."

"But what about the bond? Your mating madness is rising for her regularly? How are you supposed to be a chieftain when you're distracted in that way?"

I shook my head again, because I still didn't have an answer for that. "I've got it mostly under control."

My mother scoffed. "This is ridiculous. I'm going to talk to her. If she understands why she must remove the implant—"

"You won't go near her," I snapped. "I won't have you being hateful to her."

My mother drew herself up. "That's not fair, son."

"I am in love with this woman, and she has no one but me. I won't let you hurt her. Don't speak to her until you can be welcoming to her, if you don't mind. This woman is going to bear your grandchildren. Make your peace with it. Until then, stay away from her."

* * *

rowan

After the greeting with the people, I thought I'd meet Hugo's family, but instead, I was sent off to a room on my own and food was sent up to me. The Treebark people lived in trees, their houses hollowed out inside massive, thick trunks, the trees rising high into the sky over us. I couldn't even imagine how old these trees must be to have gotten so thick and tall. It was horrible to think of their being cut down.

After I ate, I explored the room I was in, which was modern inside, with a bathroom off of it with a shower and toilet and sink. There was even a replicator on the wall that looked capable of making human drinks like

168

coffee and hot chocolate, two things that the Toth had taken a liking to and were now available all over the galaxy.

I put away my clothes in the closet, which was half bare. The other half was full of male clothes in Hugo's size. I realized this was *our* room, and that made me feel warm and happy inside.

I thought maybe I could turn on the screen and see if there was something to watch.

But instead, I opened the door and peered out into the hallway.

No one was out there, so I stepped out and started walking around, palming the controls of doors, having them slide open, looking for Hugo.

I didn't find him, but I found a library and a sauna room and something with exercise equipment and a huge kitchen with lots of counter space.

I also ran into Hugo's sister, Kenna.

She was young, ten years younger than Hugo, he said, and he hadn't seen her since he left for the fights. When he'd gone, she'd been a little girl. Now, she was an adolescent. She was pretty and wide eyed, and she and I held a small, halting conversation, full of giggles, since she didn't speak Common and my Rrolln wasn't great either. She kept going too fast for me, and the word in Rrolln that I said the most was, "Slow. Slow."

She had beautiful gold shimmering patterns painted onto her her horns, and I complimented her on them. She told me that she got her horns done once or twice every gemoon, and invited me to come too, before realizing that I didn't have horns. Then she apologized over and over again, even though I assured her it was okay.

I told her that human women sometimes painted

their fingernails and toenails and showed her.

She showed me her claws, which were retractable, like Hugo's, and we discussed whether paint would wear off when they were retracted.

I liked her.

She was adorable and sweet to me.

But then, in the middle of the conversation, Hugo's mother showed up and she didn't look pleased.

I tried to say hello to her, but she snapped in Common, "Your mate has ordered me not to speak to you." She seized Kenna's hand and pulled her daughter away from me.

I blinked into their wake.

Hugo appeared only moments later. Noticing my expression, he made a face. "What did she say to you? My mother. I can tell she said something."

"Only that you told her not to speak to me," I said.

He groaned.

"What is it, Hugo?" I said.

"She's being horrible," he told me. "She's… she said that the Toth turned me into one of them and that now I want human women, and she's taking that out on you. I told her that the Toth oppress your kind just as much as mine, possibly worse, what with the constant rape, but she…" He clenched his hands into fists.

I put my hand on his arm. "It's okay."

"It's the opposite of okay," he said. "I wanted her to help you, to welcome you, and to teach you what you need to know about being a chieftess. I've never been a chieftess, so I don't know. None of that is happening, however, and it makes me livid."

"I guess I can see where she's coming from," I said, and I could. Hugo had been in the arena for years. I couldn't imagine what that must have been like for his mother, not knowing if he would come home at all, or if he'd be killed in the ring. "She must despise the Toth for taking you from her."

"That's not an excuse," he said. "Besides, it goes deeper than that. My father, he was forward thinking. He wanted the clan to be part of the galactic society, to move with the times. He married my mother because she represented the opposite side of the debate. She wanted to preserve our clan's culture and beliefs. It was a political marriage that probably was only as successful as it was because they somehow managed to mate to each other. It brought them together, but they never agreed. They always fought. When I went away to university, that's when she feels she lost me."

I nodded slowly, taking that in. "Is that still going on within your people, this push and pull between the outside world and your clan's traditions?"

"I've been gone for years, Rowan, but... I assume so." He touched my cheek. "You don't need to worry about this."

"If I'm the chieftess, I think I do," I said.

He feathered his fingers over my face. "How are you so... how are you exactly right for me? How can I have been so lucky to have found you?"

I swallowed. "Hugo, you say things like that, but—"

He kissed me.

I kissed back, spreading my palms out over his powerful chest, feeling the tug of everything I felt for him threatening to overtake me. But no. I pulled back. "I think we need to talk."

"Talk about what?" He traced the outline of my jaw, smiling at me.

"There's some reason you're holding back with me, and I need to know if it's just because you're afraid of hurting me, or if there's something else to it."

He let his hand drop, and his entire demeanor changed. "No matter how hard I hold back, I'm still too rough."

"You know I don't think so," I said. "And… that part of me, that part that's turned on by how forceful you are, I don't think you like it." Oh, I'd just said that out loud.

He didn't say anything. He just looked at me, blinking his dark, unhuman eyes at me.

Stupid, sometimes I was so *stupid*. This was our first night together on his home planet. His mother was making things difficult for him. He had just told me that I was right for him, that he felt lucky to be with me, and I had to go and ruin it? Why?

"I like everything about you," he said in a deep voice.

"I'm okay with, um, with it not being, um…" I lowered my voice. "Filthy or whatever. If you don't like it like that—"

"Rowan." There was a warning in his voice.

"Maybe it's not a good time to talk about this," I decided.

He sighed. "I don't have anything to say about that, no."

Right. He disapproved of me. Here he was, with his mating bond that took him over and made him forceful and intense, and he thought there was something wrong with me because I liked it that way. I felt ashamed of myself. I didn't know why I was so turned on by things like that, anyway, but I didn't mean to be, and I certainly didn't need it that way. I was fine with it being gentle and sweet. I was in love with him, and that was a sweet and gentle feeling, not… not a filthy one.

I just wished he'd stop saying that I was perfect, though, because he obviously didn't think that, not really.

But he'd been the one who said those things. He'd trapped my hands against the wall. He'd used the word filthy. He'd said I belonged to him.

So…

Well, whatever was going on with him, I thought maybe he wasn't being honest with himself, and I wasn't sure we were going to be able to avoid it forever. However, it *was* the first night here, and I wasn't going to push right now.

I patted his chest. "Okay, let's just leave that for now. We're both tired. We should go to bed."

He nodded. "Yeah. Tired." He searched my gaze.

I gave him a little smile. "Not *too* tired, of course." We always made love before we went to sleep, after all.

He drew in a noisy breath, rubbing his face against mine. "Rowan," he growled.

I pressed into him, sighing. "Hugo."

SEVENTEEN

hugo

I woke up with my body wrapped around Rowan, my hard cock burrowed in the cleft of her bare ass.

This had happened before, because we spooned while we slept a lot, and I usually woke up hard, so I was always poking her somewhere.

But this time, I woke up screaming, half in a panic, and I rolled into her, trapping her under me, my pelvis pressing down into hers.

She woke up panicked too, fear scent rolling off her. "Hugo?"

The dream was leaving me. It was a bad dream, one that left me frightened and disgusted but also half aroused. Sometimes I dreamed about the arena, but sometimes I dreamed about other things, things I'd seen the Toth do, things I'd seen other gladiators do, to… to women, usually small, helpless, naked human women like the mate in my bed.

I started apologizing in Rrolln, and I rocked off her, or I tried.

Two of my strands had attached.

"Roots and branches," I muttered. One strand was burrowed above her asshole and the other was beneath, and the head of my hard cock was lined up with—

No.

I plucked the strand out of her.

She let out a little cry, and through the other strand I felt that yanking it out had hurt her. The strands were connected to her nerves, and when they detached on their own, they came out easier.

The other strand pulsed into her, pushing her full of sensation, turning her on.

I felt that rock through me, too, her arousal feeding my arousal. My cock head spurted liquid on her opening, and I slid against her there.

She gasped. "Hugo..."

"No," I said. "That's not—" I yanked out the other strand.

She made another noise.

I threw myself over to the other side of the bed, lying on my back, panting. My whole body was on edge. The mating instinct wasn't rising, and I could only think the fear and disgust from the dream were keeping it down, because once my strands started to lock on, by all rights, I should have lost control.

She sat up next to me, twisting to look down at me.

I felt like crying.

Curse the Toth. What was *wrong* with me?

"Um..." She bit down on her lower lip. "You didn't *have* to stop, I guess?"

My lips parted and I just stared at her. I remembered once, having her from behind, the strands pulsing into her there, how we'd both been surprised she liked it. "No," I managed.

"You don't want me there?"

"Do *you* want me there?"

She shrugged. "I don't know."

I licked my lips. "Have you, uh... have you ever let someone fuck you there?"

"No." This was forceful. "I know you think I'm some kind of loose whore or something—"

"I *don't*. Please don't say that about yourself. Why would you think that I—"

"It's just that your strands can make me come from sucking you off, you know, when they're locked onto my throat, so I'm pretty sure they'd make it work, and that I'd enjoy it. You're big... you're way too big, and typically, I'd be way too scared, but the strands... I think... I don't know." She lay back down on the bed next to me. "Never mind."

We lay on the bed, both on our backs, staring at the ceiling.

"I was having this dream," I said finally.

"Oh, right," she said. "I guess I forgot that you were upset. Was it about that? Maybe that's why you didn't want to have sex?"

"You have no idea the things I've seen done to human women," I muttered. "You have no idea the number of Toth cocks I've watched be shoved into every available..." Now, I wanted to cry again. "Because they film things and they put it on screens before fights to get us... worked up. Women sobbing and bleeding and them *laughing*. And then fights, prizes at fights. Before my own fights, I've stood in the wings, doing warm-up stretches while some woman is being pounded by whatever half-bloody thing won her, and that's not even counting the other sorts of prizes. Sometimes, the handlers would get women for their gladiators, and they'd throw them to them, sometimes one woman to be shared between... I see those women sometimes, in those dreams, and I don't know if it's worse when they're crying or saying things like 'stop' and 'don't' and 'help me' or when they..." My voice broke. "When they just look dead inside, like they've switched off."

"Hugo," she whispered.

"No," I said, "the worst thing is *me*, because I dream about it, and then I wake up *hard*."

It was quiet again.

She sat back up and looked down at me. *She* was crying. One tear was trickling down her cheek. "Oh, Hugo," she breathed, "I'm so sorry. I had no idea."

I looked away from her. My throat felt scratchy. My eyes stung. No tears came.

"Can I touch you?"

"Of course," I said, but I realized I was happy she'd asked before putting her hands on me, that it was good that she'd asked.

She settled one small, warm palm in the middle of my chest, just rested it there.

"You're not… you don't *belong* to me. I don't *own* you. I don't *use* your body." My voice was strained.

"No," she assured me. "No, it's not like that at all, baby."

"But I want to," I said, grimacing. "But I like it."

"No, Hugo, it's not the same thing."

"Maybe my mother's right. Maybe I am turning into a Toth."

"*No.*"

My lower lip was starting to tremble.

She started kissing me, little soft presses of her lips all over my nose and my cheeks and my horns and my chin. "No, Hugo, please, don't, we never have to, I didn't know, I swear, I'm sorry."

I grunted and rolled us over, trapping her body under mine.

She gasped, looking up at me. There were still tears

in her eyes.

The mating instinct took this moment to rear its ugly head. I threw back my head, gritting my teeth at the ceiling. "Not now, roots and branches, not now."

She brushed fingers over my bare arms and shoulders. "It's okay, it's okay. I want you, I always want you. I love you, Hugo."

The need went off at the back of my skull like an explosion, and my strands burrowed in along with my hard cock. In hisecs, I was balls deep in her, and she was squirming and sighing against me, the strands sending me all the sensations in her body.

"I do belong to you," she whispered. "I'm yours. Take me, Hugo. Take me hard."

I grunted.

I took her.

I rutted with her like the beast I was, like the animal they'd made me.

And I liked it.

EIGHTEEN

In the morning, I wanted to talk, but Hugo was between my legs instead, licking me, which made it hard for me to think. He was unhurried and thorough, stopping only to make little exclamations about how good I tasted.

He got me off that way, which he almost never managed to do, because usually the mating instinct took him over, but I built there, his hands clutching the globes of my ass, holding me up and open for him like a feast he couldn't get enough of, and I convulsed and undulated and fell apart for him while he breathed against me as I came, praising me for it.

"That's good, Rowan, just like that. Come just like that for me. Very good." His voice was deep and measured and so affecting.

Stars, it was good.

After, we fucked, and he was more intense than usual, but it was fine because I was so stars-shined wet for him.

I came again, because of course I did, because he couldn't come unless I did when the strands were locked in, and then I was a puddle of just-fucked flesh on our bed while he was up and moving and chipper like the sunrise.

He stretched, looking out the window in our bedroom at the tree-lined horizon. In the distance, I could see icy mountains. Everything else on the planet that surrounded this strip of livable land on the equator was frozen, apparently. "I forgot how much I missed the trees," he said softly.

"Hugo, about last night," I said.

He turned and looked at me. "What about last night?"

"About… about your dream?"

"I think those nightmares are going to go away, don't you?" he said, shaking his head. "I mean, they'll fade out. They have to." He gave me a little sheepish smile. "Sorry you've got to deal with a mate who's so screwed up in the head."

"No, no, I didn't mean it like that." I wanted to hop out of bed and go to him, but my muscles barely worked. I managed to sit up.

"You're going to say I'm not screwed up?"

"Hugo, you're *not.*"

He gave me a withering look.

"Well, I'm sure that the arena…" I spread my hands. "If you ever want to tell me things that happened to you, things you saw, the way you felt… I want to listen. Don't feel like you need to hide it from me."

He looked back out the window. "No, I don't like thinking about it. I don't want to talk about it."

"But… about us having sex that's a little bit… about it making me hot when you force me —"

"*That's* how you feel?" His jaw twitched. "Forced?"

"No, obviously, I'm into it." I wrapped the sheets around my body and did get out of the bed. "I don't mean it like that."

"Yeah, you keep saying that."

I put my hand on his back. "I like it, and if you like it, too, then I don't see what the harm is in—"

"In treating you like property, got it." He shook me off.

"No, I don't mean—"

"What *do* you mean?"

"I…" I didn't finish.

"Well, if you really want to talk, you should probably figure that out." He went to the closet and started pulling clothes out of it. "Here's what I'm thinking, and I hope it's not too hard on you? If I'm away from you, the bond can't trigger, so I was thinking I'd spend most of the day trying to get caught up on all my responsibilities. We can meet up for lunch to eat, and, uh… connect."

I smirked. "Connect, okay."

He rounded on me. "Okay, we'll meet for lunch and I'll fuck your brains out, and then we'll eat. Better?"

I shook my head. "I didn't mean to make you upset."

"It's not your fault," he said, stepping into a pair of pants. "Like I was just getting done saying, I'm screwed up in the head."

"Hugo, I think it would be normal for anyone to be shaken after what you've been through."

He nodded. "I guess. Uh, anyway, then I'll see you at bedtime."

"So, what am I supposed to do while you're trying to stay away from me to keep your mating madness in control?"

"You can stay in bed and watch some vids on the screen?"

I flopped back on the bed. "I see."

"You don't like this plan?"

"It's okay for a day," I said. "But why do I get the

impression this is how you think you're going to run your life? You have to avoid me, or you fuck me constantly, so we're not going to see each other very much, are we?"

"It's for your own good," he muttered. "I don't want to hurt you."

I groaned. "Hugo, this is why we need to talk."

"We can talk until the trees touch the sky, Rowan, but I feel you through the strands, and I know if you're hurt, and you're not going to convince me otherwise." He yanked a shirt over his head and surveyed me. "Okay, but I see your point that you can't spend your life lying in bed, watching vids, and waiting around with your legs spread for me to come and fuck you, as appealing as it sounds to have you at my beck and call."

"Yes, you were opposed to treating me like your property?" I raised an eyebrow.

He lowered his head, uncomfortable. "So, it's just for today, until we can work something else out."

"Fine," I said. "Just for today."

But I didn't make it even an hour after he left me. I couldn't stand the idea of being stuck in this room all by myself when I was on a new planet and surrounded by a whole clan of Treebark people who were now *my* people.

I didn't know how to be their chieftess, and the person who did know, Hugo's mother, didn't like me, but maybe I could change her mind.

Typically, I wasn't a person who'd rush headlong into a conflict situation. It was a risk to go to her, and it might make everything worse. However, there was a real potential that it could make things better.

As far as I knew, this house was the chieftain's

family house, sort of like a castle or a manor or something. It didn't look like a castle, but then all the houses just looked like hollow trees from the outside.

So, maybe if I just walked around the house and looked into rooms like I'd been doing the night before, I'd run into Hugo's mother.

I realized I didn't even know her name.

Wow, of all the things to not know before going into a possibly volatile conversation with a person who didn't like me, this was probably one of the worst.

I should have given up on the idea.

But, I mean, I *am* stupid sometimes. Maybe a lot of the times.

I found her coming out of the exercise room. She was a little sweaty, so she'd probably just got done exercising.

That was my second stroke of bad luck. She was probably in the mood for a shower, not to talk to me.

She saw me, and her posture changed. She squared her feet and lifted her chin. It looked like a challenge to me.

I tried a smile. "I know Hugo said we shouldn't talk." I said this in Common, because she'd spoken to me in it last night. I didn't trust myself to have a conversation with as much nuance as this would require in Rrolln. "But he also told me why you're upset, and I have to say I understand."

She snorted. "Oh, do you?"

"The Toth have taken much from everyone," I said. "They abducted my grandparents and kept them in a lab to study them, like animals. My grandparents are lucky to have lived."

"You're from that Colony, then?"

Where did she think I was from? Humans all came

from there these days, since the wormhole was closed. I nodded. "Well, my parents were. I was born away from there. They wanted to be part of the galaxy, not to live stifled with their own kind."

"Did they."

Wrong thing to say, considering she was on the side of keeping her people free from the taint of the offworlders. "I mean, they're both dead now, so I don't know how it worked out for them."

"They did not teach you to value your culture," she said.

"No," I said. "I didn't have a culture, though, and I… I'm drawn to the idea of that. I love it here, actually, and everything that Hugo's told me about the Treebark people and your clan, it really enthralls me. I want you to know that I respect you, and that I'm not here to try to change things. I want to be part of your traditions, not to alter them."

She snorted. "Our traditions are for us. You're human. You can't be part of them."

"Couldn't you let me try?" I took a step toward her. "Hugo said that you would be the one who would teach me the duties of a chieftess, and I want to learn. Maybe there's something that I could do to show you. Some way you could give me a chance to prove myself?"

She ran a finger over the tip of one of her horns, which were decorated in silvery patterns. "Well, there is the Roots Gala coming up. It's a religious ceremony and celebration that is usually hosted by the chieftess. She sees to the food and the music and the decorations."

I raised my eyebrows. "Okay." I had been thinking of something smaller, but planning a gala, sure, why not? "I'd be honored to be given that kind of responsibility. It would mean a lot to me that you'd trust me with something sacred like that. I... wow."

She nodded. "Yes, it's meant to be very elaborate. The decorations especially. And the music should be quite exuberant, lots of current dance tunes."

For a religious ceremony? Really.

She was still talking. "I can't wait to see what you come up with. I'll be sure to tell everyone it's all been up to you."

"Well," I said, forcing myself to smile. "I'm so glad that we were able to come to a compromise so quickly."

"Oh, yes," she said. "And I must say, I think it's intelligent, what you're doing, using birth control to make sure that you don't become pregnant with my son's child. Why get yourself so deeply in when you can't be sure it's going to work out?"

"He told you about that?" Of course he did. I thought it was private, between the two of us, but I guessed he would need to explain why we weren't going off on the little mating retreat that we should traditionally do.

"My son and I are still close," she said. "Despite what the Toth have done to him, he is still my flesh and blood."

"Of course he is," I said.

She let out a sigh. "Well, I need to get in a shower, I think, if you don't mind excusing me?"

"I wouldn't want to keep you," I said. "I'm very sorry. Please." I gestured.

She moved past me, and I didn't like the smile on her face.

The first thing I did was to go and find that library I'd seen. The books were there, all preserved, behind glass. The text had all been scanned and was accessible by screen. I used the database to look up any books with information about the Roots Gala.

Yes, just as I thought, it was a very somber affair, held every year to commemorate the passing of loved ones in the years past. It was hosted by the chieftess, but if I had done elaborate decorations and jaunty dance music, I would have offended every single member of the clan.

Did she think I was an idiot?

I fumed.

She must, or she wouldn't have said something so ridiculous. She wouldn't think that I would have done what she said, would she? Certainly, she'd think that I'd ask Hugo about it.

Maybe she had never spoken much to her mate since they'd argued about everything, or maybe she thought that Hugo didn't talk to me but just used me for sex, since she assumed Hugo was badly influenced by the Toth.

That made me think of what had happened the night before, what he'd told me.

It made me fume even harder. She had put that idea in his head. Not entirely, of course. He obviously did have bad associations with all kinds of things he'd seen in the arena, and my heart went out to him. That life, the threat of constant violence, the exposure to everything he'd seen, the fact that he must have thought that any hidosec he could die, and that he'd never even get a chance to have sex again, and then to be watching all that…

I knew what kind of galaxy we lived in.

I knew how bad it was.

And Hugo wasn't bad. He wasn't anything like the

Toth. He was a good man. How dare his mother make him question himself?

My first inclination was to march through the house until I found him and tell him everything. Then I'd soothe him and reassure him that his mother was wrong about it all, that I knew him, and that whatever turned me on, I *was* turned on. It was different.

Of course, if I found him, the first thing that would happen would be that he would jump me.

We'd fuck, and I didn't know if he was alone or not. He might not be. The mating bond didn't care about that. It could end up being really embarrassing and awkward. He'd wanted to stay away from me, and there was a reason.

Furthermore, he'd told his mother not to speak to me, and I'd forced her into it. I should have trusted his assessment of the woman.

And I was going to somehow have to make peace with her. She wasn't going anywhere. I didn't need to drive a further wedge between him and his mother. I needed to find some way to make everything better.

So, to that end, I was just going to make the best Roots Gala that the Treebark people had ever seen, and I was never even going to mention the fact that she'd tried to make me screw up.

As for the other thing she'd said, about the birth control implant, well... of course she didn't want me pregnant. She wanted to get rid of me.

I marched into the bathroom and rolled up my sleeve. There was the little port, just above my elbow. I rummaged around until I found a set of tweezers in one of the drawers, and then I pinched the port until I could see the strands of the implant.

I seized them with the tweezers and yanked.

The implant came out, taking the port with it, leaving a tiny little wound on my arm. I bandaged it.

I looked down at the implant, which was just a small thing. My heart pounded.

Well.

Just did that.

About me being impulsive?

Yeah.

NINETEEN

hugo

At lunch, Rowan was not in our bedroom, where I'd told her to wait for me.

I sent a message to her bracelet and she sent back, *I assumed we were eating in the dining room.*

I sent back, *Considering what I'm going to do to you the hisec I get close?*

We can lock the doors, right?

I went to the dining room. She was setting a complete traditional Treebark person soup setting, all the utensils in the right place, with the proper glassware and everything. I just shook my head at it, stunned.

"I screwed it up," she said. "I asked Kenna to look, and she said it was right, but I know you can't always trust the information you get in books, and—"

"It's perfect." I was flabbergasted. I pulled her into an embrace, kissing her cheekbone, then her jaw. "You smell different."

She wriggled around to put her arms around me. "I do? Well, maybe it's the assortment of soaps here? Reminds you of home? Do I smell like an Abbunian?"

"You smell…" I ran my nose up and down her neck. I didn't know, but it wasn't soap, and I liked it. I put my mouth on hers.

She beamed at me. "It's not a bad smell, then? And you like the soup setting?"

I kissed her again.

She gasped against my lips. "If you're going to bend me over the table, just be careful not to knock everything over."

I laughed, pulling away. "No, we can eat."

She looked at me, eyebrows raised. "No crazed mating madness?"

"Uh..." I kissed her again. "No, it's..." The smell, it was affecting me, but it was a different sort of affect. I felt aroused and aware of her, but not out of control. "How did you do all this?"

"I used the replicator for some of it." She pulled away to look at the table. "But I read that this was the traditional meal that's served at the Roots Gala, and I wanted to give it a try first, since I'm going to host it."

"Wait. What?"

"Well, I know you told me to stay in our room and not to talk to your mother, but I went looking for her, and I talked her into letting me do it. It's a traditional chieftess responsibility, right?"

"It's next fogemoon," I said. "How are you going to have time to—"

"Well, I have nothing else to do." She shrugged. She gave me a little laugh. "I don't want to screw it up, though. Maybe if there's someone else you could introduce me to who might be able to give me some pointers?"

"Uh..." I nodded. "Yeah, I'll take care of that."

"Some woman you've had sex with, since you've had sex with everyone in the clan," she said.

I laughed. "I'll see if I can dig someone up who was already mated when my mother went on her rampage and threw me at every eligible girl."

"Your mother did it? Eew." She made a face. Then she took a deep breath. "No, no, I'm trying to be fair with your mother. No more thoughts like that."

"You're..." I looked around again. "You're so perfect. You're too perfect."

"I wish you would stop saying that." She looked at me, shaking her head. "Especially when you... when we..." Her hand caressed my chest. "We have stuff to work through, Hugo. It's not perfect."

"Yes, it is," I said, wrapping my arms around her. "Let's eat."

The soup was quite good, I thought. Some of the ingredients that had come from the replicator had a bit of a plastic taste, but replicated food was always like that. I spent the entire meal astonished, saying, "You did this? You cooked this? Did you ever tell me you could cook? Could you have been cooking on the ship the whole way here?"

And she just laughed and said there was nothing to cook on the ship, that it had been all rations bars and ready-made meals.

It was true the ship hadn't had a replicator.

My mating bond didn't rise once during lunch, but I wanted her, and afterwards, I did bend her over the table, but by then, her scent had changed again. When I got her pants off, she was bleeding.

"Stars," she said. "I guess I knew that would happen, but I thought we'd have a day or two. Of course it just started right away. Stupid period."

I was confused.

Then we had a long conversation about how human female's cycles worked, and it was different than Treebark people females, who only bled if they ovulated and weren't fertilized, which happened, of course, but was, well, was different.

"I mean, this is part of why I wanted to keep the implant in," she said. "Because then, no period, and of course, the hisec I take it out, it starts. Are you really grossed out?"

"You took out the implant?"

"Oh," she said. "Yeah."

"You didn't think to mention that?"

"I was going to, I just…" She shrugged.

I kissed her. Really hard. "That's huge that you did that. You didn't have to."

"I know," she said. "I honestly… I'm a little freaked."

"No wonder your scent changed," I said. "And the mating madness must not be rising, because you're not fertile." I grinned.

"But that doesn't make sense," she said. "Because I wasn't fertile when the implant was in."

"Yeah, I don't think my body can sense technology, but I'm attuned to you naturally, so, uh…"

"So, no bending me over the table," she said, sounding wistful.

"Wait, do you want to?" I said. "Does it hurt you while you're, uh, in the period?"

"*On* my period," she corrected, grinning. "No, it doesn't hurt. You're not grossed out?"

"Definitely not," I said.

"But will the strands lock on?"

"Yeah, of course," I said. "You sure? Because women of my kind, when they're not fertile, they're usually not… into it."

"Why are human women so popular?" she said, spreading her hands and giving me a little wink.

I swallowed.

We gazed at each other, and something passed between us in our expressions.

"Okay," I breathed finally. "Turn around, then, Rowan. Put your arms out and your cheek flat into the table. Spread your legs for me."

She did it, and I could hear the way her breath hitched.

I unfastened my fly. "You want my cock, don't you?"

"Yes," she whispered.

I was hard and I put it up against her, but without the madness rising, I didn't have to take her so fast. I could wait a little. I put my mouth to the back of her neck, and reached around her to lift her from the table a little. I rubbed her nipples stiff.

She sighed.

"That good?"

"So good," she said. "But not as good as your cock. You're teasing me with it, Hugo."

"You really want it?"

"You want me to beg you?" she said in a knowing sort of voice.

I grunted.

"Hugo, please," she said. "I want you to take me. Make me yours."

I seized her hips, digging my fingers into her skin. This was probably wrong, playing this way, letting her say stuff like that, but it really turned me on, and I didn't stop her.

"Please fuck me? Please put your big, pretty cock in me? I need it."

I slid the tip of her inside.

She moaned. "More."

"More, huh?" I said.

"Please," she sighed. "Maybe that's the kind of girl I am. A greedy girl."

I grunted, pushing even more deeply into her. My strands started to slowly burrow in, one at a time.

Each one wrenched a cry from her.

"Greedy Rowan," I said. "Beg me for the rest of my cock."

"Please, Hugo, fuck me, make me come on your hard cock, *please*?"

One of my strands found her clit, and we both felt it.

We gasped together.

"There you go," I said, starting to thrust in her. "Better?"

"Much," she moaned, thrusting her hips back against me.

I loved how it felt. I loved that I had control over my muscles, that I wasn't just a slave to my instinct, that my body wasn't just mating on its own. The mating bond was overwhelming and intense, and there was a great deal of pleasure from it, but this… this was good. I wanted her like this.

I wanted her again and again.

The strands still made us aware of each other's pleasure, but they weren't sending sensations into me and altering my body to better please her, which was both good and bad at the same time, I thought, because on the one hand, usually, when I fucked her, she was *right there*, pretty much ready to explode, and I couldn't say I hated that, but on the other hand, I wanted to understand her body and to know how to please her myself.

And so we settled into a long stretch of experimental movement as I dragged myself in and out of her and moved to stretch the strands.

Finally, I reached around, put my fingers between her legs, and rubbed her.

She let out these amazing hoarse cries when I started making circles around her clit, and I felt her pleasure come through the strands like a low smolder that burned brighter and brighter.

I figured out—trial and error—feeling it through the strands, how to angle myself to the right spot, so that I was pushing and tugging her from the inside, fingers and cock and strands all at once, and then she was *there* again, and my cock started to slowly get there too.

Mating bond or not, I didn't come unless she did, so I had a vested interest in getting her there, but I liked that.

Truthfully, when there wasn't a bond with a woman, it was always stressful. It was reassuring knowing that she enjoyed it as much as I did, and having done it myself, having figured it out, this made me feel better, and I was even more turned on as we moved together.

When she came—a roar of flames that licked through her body—the sensation traveled through the strands and lit me up. I felt it burrow into my balls and then to the base of my cock. I went tighter, harder, rock hard, and then I let go too.

Then we were just a gasping tangle of limbs on the table, and I didn't think I'd ever felt quite as in love with her as I did right then.

TWENTY

rowan

If I needed more reason to think that Hugo was too good to be real, he was the happiest he'd ever been that I was on my period. It didn't faze him at all. He seemed even more interested in me, and he spent way more time on foreplay.

At some point, it was a little too much for me, when I was heavy, and he was disappointed that I was turning him down until I suggested we could try it in the shower, and then we were in the shower for half the day.

Even though he was supposed to be dealing with his responsibilities during the day, he hadn't been. He was just fucking me all the time, and he didn't even have the bond to blame. I had to admit that without the urgency of the bond, he was gentler, and the sex was less brutal, and—even though it was exciting for him to want me that much—there was a different quality to this coupling, which wasn't forced in any way, and that made it much more affecting.

I wondered at that. The bond had brought us close, yes, but our own choices were what had sealed us together.

We weren't sure what was going to happen with his mating madness, but if it really was attuned to me, then it might only flare up when I was fertile, and that was really only for the six or so days leading up to my ovulation, maybe a fogemoon of every moon-cycle. Hugo wanted this to happen badly, and I guessed I wanted it too. I couldn't honestly decide, because I didn't want Hugo avoiding me during the madness. I didn't want him to be worried about hurting or breaking me. I wanted him close like this. On the other hand, having all this sex with Hugo meant I was effectively kept from doing anything else.

Hugo spent time in between bouts of sex researching my cycle, which he found fascinating, and I spent all the time trying to figure out the Roots Gala. Some of it I could take care of by walking down the hallway in his house, like going to make sure that there were enough plastorches for the ceremony in the clan's storage.

But I needed to go and meet with people to set up the rest of it, and Hugo was completely dominating my attention.

My period ebbed out and Hugo's attentions only got more intense.

Now, he started using his tongue on my pussy again, and we both liked that, and that became a prelude to almost every sexual session. He would lick me all over, teasing my nipples into stiff peaks before delving between my thighs and licking me into a tongue-swirling frenzy until I came, and then his strands would lock on and he'd slip easily into my slick passage and we'd move together, and it was *good*.

Honestly, when we made love those times, I started feeling like we were melding into each other, as cliche as it sounds. I'd always had a bit of a sensation like that with him, even the first time in the arena. I got confused as to where each of us ended when we were tangled up, but it was becoming several times as intense, and the strands only cemented it, because I could feel his pleasure as well.

At first, it had been like an echo, but now, sometimes it was confusing, and I felt as if his cock was part of my body, or I felt his hands on me as if they were my own. When we were joined, we merged, and the sensation was so powerful and so overwhelming that it awed me.

Sometimes, we'd break apart, both a little sweaty and gasping, and we'd breathe together, in the same rhythm, and as I would stare at his face—which was dear to me in this way that almost hurt—I would get the sensation that this connection between us was almost mystical, and I felt reverence toward it.

At the same time, it all seemed fragile to me in a way I couldn't quite understand.

The closer we got, the more something at the back of my mind rustled and made me nervous, as if something was coming, something bad.

But I ignored it.

I didn't know what it was.

And sometimes I was stupid. This was good. I didn't want to ruin it, not the way I ruined everything.

Hugo had promised me that he would find someone to help me out with the Roots Gala and with my duties in general, and he'd sought a woman named Rrila out, even set up a time for me to meet her, but then he kept canceling it and rescheduling it, which was driving me crazy.

When I tried to argue with him about it, he'd distract me with sex.

This was both driving me nuts and also creating a lot of stress for me, because this Gala was important to me. I hadn't seen Hugo's mother since she'd lied to me about the gala, but then I hadn't seen anyone. Even so, I wanted to do this right, and I had to prove to this woman that I wasn't going to destroy all her traditions and ruin everything that was important to her.

One night, I woke up to voices.

Hugo was outside the door of our bedroom, talking to his mother, who was saying that if he wasn't going to do any of his duties, he should take me and go on a proper noccht.

Hugo told her that should wait until I was actually fertile and his mating bond triggered again, and his mother had been disgusted with him.

"If you're not feeling regular mating madness, then what is keeping you from your duties? If she can't even become pregnant—"

"This is not something I want to talk about with you, Mother," said Hugo, obviously embarrassed.

"You are a chieftain, Hugo," said his mother. "Maybe if you were some cavalier Toth nobleman, you could spend all your time with your human plaything—"

"She is my *mate*," Hugo snapped. "Never say that about her again."

But the next morning, Hugo did not cancel my meeting with Rrila. He gave me his earpiece, which he'd modified for me so that it would assist me in speaking and understanding Rrolln.

I wasn't sure if I should talk to him about what his mother had said. I didn't, and it was because whenever I started to, that thing that was rustling in the back of my mind rustled louder. I didn't want to poke whatever all that was.

Anyway, I had other things to concentrate on.

Rrila lived in another tree trunk, across the clearing

from Hugo's. Inside, it was much smaller, with only a few rooms carved out, though all of them had technological amenities and were clean, tidy, and tastefully decorated.

Well, there was a pile of toys on the floor of the lounge room, where a little Treebark boy was on his hands and knees, face tilted in a way to get a perfect view of the little toy animal that he was making dance around. He was adorable, murmuring in a low voice as he pretended with his toy.

Rrila's belly was swollen with another child and her mate hovered nearby when I arrived.

She put a hand on his chest and told him that she was fine, and that she had everything she needed, and that she would tell him if there was anything else.

After he ambled off to the lounge room with their child, Rrila laughed. "Sometimes the bond is a bit smothering, but I suppose it's better than the alternative." She and I were in the kitchen, sitting on either side of an island that seemed to serve both as counter space and as a table.

"Smothering?" I said. "Alternative?"

She waved that away, smiling. "No, no, don't mind me. We have other things to talk about, don't we? And is that your voice or is it a bot?"

I showed her the earpiece and we chatted about that for a while.

Then we got down to business and talked about the Roots Gala.

She informed me that Hugo had come to her, because—while the gala was technically the purview of the chieftess—Hugo's mother had attempting to be both chieftain and chieftess for the past several years, and she hadn't been able to fulfill all of the duties on her own. Rrila had been essentially putting together the gala for years now, but what with her pregnancy, she was glad that I was here to take it over.

Of course, it was taking place in a matter of days, and she thought it was a bit strange I was just getting to it at the last hidosec.

"I guess you're at a bit of a different stage in the bond, though," she said, winking at me. "I'm amazed he let you out of his sight."

I blushed.

She called her mate back in. His name was Gonn, and she gave him a rundown of the things we'd talked about. She told him that if he could organize some of the men in the clan to bring in supplies for us and to help with the setup, there would be credits for them, because Hugo had authorized me to do that.

Gonn furrowed his brow. "How many men?"

"Credits," said Rrila. "Certainly you won't have trouble gathering enough men to help. What are they doing besides traveling out to the tavern on the other side of the lagoon anyway?"

Gonn looked away, uncomfortable. He shoved his hands in his pockets.

Rrila gave me an embarrassed look, and then got up and went to her mate. She put her hand on his arm and spoke to him, too low for me to understand. He kissed her and they gave each other a look, one that reminded me of Hugo and me, that sort of look that seemed to say that they were in perfect sync with each other, that they were connected. Then she shooed him out the door and rubbed her neck with one hand, resting her hand on her belly with the other hand.

I realized I hadn't been asking the right sort of questions about the clan, had I? "Is there a need for credits amongst families in the clan?"

She turned to me. "I... we're doing fine." She gestured around at her house. "I have a little business making candies from tree sap. Gonn takes me to the city to ship things out several times a gemoon. It's better now that he triggered for me again. At first, I thought I couldn't manage being pregnant again, but he's much more attentive now, because of the bond." She gave me a smile.

"But other families?" I furrowed my brow.

"We don't need credits," said Rrila. "The lagoon still has fish, and we can feed ourselves as we always did. We have hollowed out shelters here amongst the trees. We..."

"But credits are necessary for installing plaslights or for the fuel to heat your homes," I said. "These are technological homes, and... how are you paying for this? With your candy business?"

She nodded.

"Does everyone have some little business like that? Selling to offworlders?"

"Not everyone," she said. "And I'd thank you not to speak too loudly of my little business, if you don't mind."

"Because the chieftess wouldn't like it," I said. How did I still not know Hugo's mother's *name*?

"Chieftess Agna has the people's best interests at heart, and she does not wish to upend our traditions."

Agna! Finally. "But what's her solution for credits?"

Rrila didn't say anything.

I stepped closer to her. "Listen, I know I'm human, and I've got this thing here to augment my voice so that we can even speak at all, but I want you to understand that I'm not an outsider. I'm your chieftain's mate, and

I'm here to help. You can speak freely with me, I promise. You can trust me. I'm in a position to help you, to make things better, but I need to know what you need."

Rrila drew in a deep breath and then let it out noisily. She sat down next to me. "Well, here is the truth, then. The men in the clan, many of them feel useless, because they don't feel as if they are capable of providing for their mates and children in the way they wish to. Certainly, we are not starving and we have shelter. When the former chieftain was in charge, things were changing."

"You mean Hugo's father?"

"Yes," she said. "Now, I sometimes wonder if he would have gone too far, left to his own devices, but with Chieftess Agna balancing him out, it was a give and take between them. There has been no progress in years, not since his death. And she has become even more entrenched since Chieftain Hugo was taken. For instance, there is a strip of trees to the southern part of our clan's holdings?"

"Yes, I heard about this. They want to cut down the trees and develop the land. They want to buy it from the clan?" I had already decided I was against this idea, but now I was beginning to wonder if I was seeing it clearly.

"Yes, you do know," she said. "Well, we would not sell the land or allow outsiders to cut down the trees, but there was a contingent of men from the clan who wanted to possibly begin cutting some of our trees down themselves. We have a special ceremony that we do before cutting down a tree, to move the souls through the root system elsewhere. I don't believe there are souls in the trees, but the ceremony also allows for sustainability and it requires a new tree to be planted in its place, so I would not change it. If the men followed this, they could cut down a small number of trees. They could have then started their own lumber business and sold the wood, which is in high demand in the closest city, but is currently being shipped in from offworld because there's no infrastructure to get it from on planet. All of that money is going off Abbunia, when it could be staying here, with us. And the clan could be benefiting."

"I suppose that the chieftess was against this idea."

"The trees belong to the clan. She would not give permission for any of the trees to be cut down." Rrila looked away. "Gonn is a good man, but even a good man gets depressed when he feels he's worthless. The bond connects him to me and gives him purpose, but before the bond, he was just as the others, drinking away the afternoon at the tavern."

"I see," I said thoughtfully.

"I'm sorry," she said. "None of this is important, truly. You came to talk to me about the Roots Gala, and you don't want to listen to me complain."

"No, it's not complaining," I said. "This is a real issue, and it's complicated, but there must be some sort of compromise. Do I have your permission to speak to Hugo about it? I won't repeat anything you don't want me to say, and I can keep your name out of it, if you like."

"Well, who else have you talked to in the clan?"

"True," I said, sitting up straight. "Perhaps I need to remedy that. How do I get to this tavern?"

* * *

hugo

When I found Rowan at the tavern, sitting at a table

with five men from my clan, listening intently as she was curled around a bottle of Abbunian beer, my first feeling was relief.

I rushed over to her. I'd been worried. She had been gone a long time, and I looked all over. I had found her bracelet, but I hadn't found her. Rrila wasn't answering messages on her own bracelet, and I started to think something horrible had happened to both of them.

But then Rrila finally got back in touch with me and told me Rowan went to the tavern, and I…

Well, I remembered when we were back on Kalion, and she'd wanted to go out and drink and dance, even though there were bots looking for her and trying to take her to jail. Maybe it wasn't exactly out of character for her.

It was weird, because I was in love with this woman, and she was the most important thing in the galaxy to me, and yet, when stuff like this happened, it made me feel like I wasn't even sure who she *was*.

She saw me and grinned. "Hugo!" She sounded a little drunk. "Pull up a chair. Grab a beer."

"You left your bracelet at home," I said.

"Did I?" She cringed. "Sorry."

Now, I was next to her. I did not pull up a chair. I glared down at her.

"Oh, you're annoyed," she said.

"I'm—" But I smelled her, and I felt the mating madness. It was different than before, and I couldn't say why that was. Maybe because of her relative fertility, or because I'd never had it trigger when she wasn't on the birth control. I didn't know. It was both more intense and less intense, as odd as that sounds.

Maybe it was me. Maybe I was getting used to it.

She sensed it, somehow. She got up so fast that she

knocked over her chair, her eyes wide.

I was fighting it, trying to push it back down my spine, which I could sometimes do.

Her gaze flitted around the room, settling for a hisec on the bathrooms, then then the front door. "Go," she said to me. "I'll follow you." She turned back to the table of men. "Sorry, we're, um, we need…" Her face reddened.

The guys at the table all got it, and they started laughing the way men do in these sorts of situations, and then… then I was angry for some reason.

So, I reached out and grabbed her by the arm and tugged her against me. "Go?" I whispered fiercely in her ear. "Why, when this is just like you like it?"

She struggled, pulling away from me. "Not this again. I do *not*." She started across the room.

I went after her. I caught her again, banding my arm around her waist, running my nose along her neck. "You probably want me to splay you out on the table and go at you right there in front of them."

"No!" She elbowed me.

I let go of her, not because she hurt me, but because I scented her fear scent, and it shamed me.

Maybe it calmed the mating madness, too. Didn't used to, but we were better bonded now, and maybe…

She took off again, running for the door.

I ran my hand over one of my horns, watching her go. I glanced back at the table of men, who weren't laughing anymore, but eyeing me in a way I didn't like. It was as though I wasn't one of them, as though I was some alien thing. It reminded me far too much of the way the audience looked at me in the ring.

I sneered at them and then I went after Rowan.

She was disappearing between the trees, on the path

that led around the lagoon and back to the village.

I went after her.

She glanced over her shoulder at me.

I put my head down. Now, I felt like I was stalking her, like I really *was* a beast, and she was… I don't know… prey.

This was fucked up.

She turned around and went faster.

I scented her on the breeze, and she still smelled like fear, but there were other things mixed in — anger and arousal.

This was turning her on, too.

She picked up the pace.

I did too.

We went that way for a while, the lagoon on one side, reflecting back the blue-green fronds of trees and the violet sky, and the dense forest on the other side, thick trunks of trees.

I got closer.

Abruptly, she veered off the path and into the woods. She was going even faster now.

I followed her, and I was gaining on her. It really wasn't a contest. She was smaller than me, and her legs were not nearly as long, and if I wanted to catch her, I could.

So, I did.

She was out of breath.

I pushed her back into a tree trunk.

She looked up at me, her breath coming in gasps, her chin jutting out. "Why do you think I like being watched? I don't."

"Fine," I said. "You don't. But you still like all the worst things about me."

"I don't. It's not that way."

"Take off your shirt and show me your tits," I said.

She let out a disbelieving noise, shaking her head at me. Her anger scent was coming off her in waves. And she did it. She yanked her shirt off and hurled it into my face.

I pulled it away and tossed it over my shoulder. "Touch your nipples."

"What is this?" she said. "Is this the mating madness? Is this—"

"This is *me*," I said in a low, hard voice. "You belong to me, now do it."

She did. But she was shaking. "What brought this on, Hugo?"

"I don't know," I said. "Maybe I just realized that I've got to be fooling myself. I want to believe this is some perfect love story, but something in you, Rowan, it's fucked up."

"What?" She squeezed her breasts with both of her hands. "Why are you saying this to me?"

"If you wanted to go and get drunk and hang out with other men, you could have just said something. You didn't have to wait until you were alone and then sneak off."

"*That's* what you think I was doing?"

I stepped closer to her, knocking her hands away from her breasts. I licked one of them.

She let out a moan. "Hugo, this is… confusing. If we're going to talk—"

"It isn't what you were doing? What? If you wanted me to fuck you in front of them—"

"I just want to *matter*, Hugo, that's all. I like it when people notice me, but it's not about sex." She gasped again, as I licked her other breast. "I was trying… there are issues with your clan, and I want…" She groaned as

I continued to lick her.

I unfastened her fly and yanked down her pants, baring her entirely. "You like attention?"

"Is that… bad?" She bit down on her lip.

I didn't say anything. I was looking at her body, and my mating madness was rising again. "Is that why you like it when I tell you what to do? Or when I hurt you? It makes you feel important?"

"I don't like being hurt."

"Yes, you do." The madness was rising faster and faster. I reached down and picked her up, balancing her against the tree.

She wrapped her legs around my hips helpfully, her breath shallow. "No, I don't. I don't know why you're so idiotic about this—"

"You liked it when I called you names too," I said. I was out of breath too. The madness was there, but it wasn't exploding. Instead, it was seeping into my skull, taking me over bit by bit. Eventually, I'd claw through my pants, rip them off and take her, but not yet.

"I don't know what you're talking about," she breathed, her chest heaving, her pretty breasts quivering.

I wormed a finger between her bodies and nudged her clit. "I called you filthy, and I felt you react through the strands."

"Hugo, that's not—"

"I called you a slut and the word almost made you come."

She let out a little noise and her pussy actually jerked against my finger.

"That's what I mean by fucked up," I rasped, because I was hard and throbbing inside my pants, and my cock wanted nothing more than to be back inside her.

"It's not. It's normal."

"You signed up for the arena, because you wanted to be used."

"No, no, I was desperate." She was moving her hips against my hand on her, and her voice had that thick, turned-on quality.

My voice was dark too. "And I want to use you. That's what we have here, between us, Rowan. We both watched too much Toth porn."

"Fuck you, Hugo," she said, her voice breaking.

"You want me to use your pussy right now?"

She moaned.

"Beg me, then," I said in a hard voice, and I wasn't sure if it was me saying this or the seeping mating bond, somehow, if it had taken control of my voice, even though I knew it couldn't really do that.

"Hugo," she panted.

"Beg me for my cock, slut," I gasped.

"Give it to me," she said through clenched teeth. "You fucking gratts, fuck me right now."

"Say it," I said. "Say what you are."

"Your slut. Your filthy slut, *please*."

My whole body went taut and needy, and I kissed her. She was unfastening my pants. I helped her, ripping my clothes.

"Fuck your slut now, Hugo," she whimpered.

And then I was inside her, and the strands were locked on, the mating madness was full throttle, and she scalded me, gripping my aching cock, and I was saying things to her, horrible things, like "take it and like it," and she was saying "please, more" and we were falling apart.

We were lost, skittering off into space with no tether,

pieces of space flotsam spinning wildly as we were jettisoned.

We had shattered somehow, both of us, and there was nothing now but brutal thrusts and ferocious pleasure.

And she came, roots and branches, the way she came, it was… it was obscene for her to come that hard after what I'd just said to her and done to her. It horrified me and electrified me and I came too, some kind of rocket take off of an orgasm that left me wrung out and used up.

When it was done, I set her down as gently as I could, and I gathered up her clothes and gave them to her.

And then I stalked off into the darkness and left her alone.

TWENTY-ONE

I rummaged through the drawers in the bathroom until I found the implant I'd taken out of myself. I didn't even know why I'd kept it. I couldn't put it back in. It wouldn't work. It had been implanted by a medical professional.

I stared at it.

I kind of wanted to cry.

I couldn't, though. For whatever reason, the waterworks were just not coming on. Anyway, whatever, it didn't matter. I wasn't sure if Hugo's madness had triggered out there in the woods. He'd been pretty forceful with me, but he'd also done a lot of talking, and he was usually not great at talking when the madness was riding him.

The only reason it might matter, truly, was that it might mean I was fertile, and that maybe he'd knocked me up.

But even if he had, that was definitely no reason to stay on this planet.

I *was* stupid.

Stars, I was stupid. And pathetic. What kind of woman signs up for the arena? Hugo was right about me. I *was* fucked up.

But, well, it didn't matter.

Just because I'd made stupid decisions in the past didn't mean I had to keep making them.

I shoved the implant into my pocket, and I went out through the hallways of the house.

Kenna was in the exercise room.

"Hey," I said. "Do you know where your mother is? I want to talk to her."

Kenna raised her eyebrows. "Seriously?"

I was going to miss Kenna. I gave her a sad smile. "I'm really sorry we didn't get to know each other better. You seem really great, honestly."

She was confused. "Um, thanks?"

I just smiled.

"You really want to talk to my mother?"

"I really do."

"I think she's in the lounge on the bottom floor."

"Thanks," I said.

Sure enough, I found Chieftess Agna scrutinizing a lap screen, pursing her lips, perched on the edge of a chair in the lounge.

She was surprised to see me.

"It's your lucky day," I said. "I want to get off Abbunia. Think you can help me with that?"

She got up quickly, clutching the screen to her chest. "What's happened?"

"Nothing," I said, shaking my head. "It's been this way all along, but I don't think either of us wanted to face it." But I couldn't continue. Now, tears were rising in my throat, when I didn't want them to, because I didn't want to cry in front of this woman. I drew in a calming breath and composed myself. "This was never going to work with Hugo and me. I was fooling myself to think it could."

"Oh," she said, and then she just stared at me,

blinking several times, seemingly stunned.

"Can you help me or not?" I said.

She carefully set down her screen. "Since you're coming to me, I assume you're not speaking to my son?"

"I would speak to him, sure," I said. "But he's not here, is he?" I gestured around at the room.

"You smell as though the two of you were recently —"

"Oh, seriously, why can all of you smell everything?" I cringed.

"I don't need to know any particulars about that, of course," she said. "I only find it a little curious, because I hope it's not because of something within the mating bond. You might not understand that our males don't entirely have control over —"

"I do," I snapped. "I understand that spectacularly well, actually."

"Oh." She cringed. "If there was an incident —"

"There was not an incident," I said.

She raised her eyebrows, clearly unconvinced.

"Or… even if there was, the incident is not the… It's *everything*, okay? I was hiding from it before. I didn't want it to be true, but now I see it, and every aspect of our entire relationship has been…" I wanted to cry again. My lower lip trembled, and I bit down on it to stop that from happening.

"Maybe you should talk to him before you go?"

I gaped at her. "What? I thought you'd be overjoyed to get rid of me."

She nodded slowly. "Yes, so did I. It's very strange I'm reacting this way." She sighed. "My son… I love him, but he can be… deep down, he's a good man. And I hesitate to say what could have happened to him in that arena during all those years. If there's anyway you might excuse him? I know some behavior is inexcusable, but he… I think he's quite taken with you, and if I let you leave, he'll be shattered. I think, if I help you, he might never forgive me."

I scoffed. "I don't believe this."

She shrugged, looking chagrined.

I licked my lips. "You lied to me about the Roots Gala."

"Oh, you figured that out?" She looked down at her shoes.

"You won't let the men in the clan start their own lumber business, even if they use a ceremony to cut down the trees?"

She raised her gaze to mine. "How do you know about that?"

"I spent all afternoon with the men at the tavern," I said. "They just want something to do, something meaningful. They want to *matter*, do you understand that? And this clan, you're trying to keep everyone locked up in a time that doesn't even exist anymore. I know the galaxy has gone downhill in a lot of ways, and the Toth are… well, there are a *lot* of problems, but… we don't solve them by standing still. We can't just shut out the rest of the galaxy and pretend that nothing has changed, because it has. And what's more important, anyway? This abstract idea of a clan or the individual clan members themselves, who are struggling and depressed and —"

"All right," she said, glaring at me. "Fine, I'll help you get off the planet. Just shut up, if you don't mind."

I crossed my arms over my chest. I pressed my lips together in a sullen line.

TWENTY-TWO

I saw the land transporter take off from the garage of my house as I was coming back from the lagoon, and I couldn't figure out who was on it or where they might be going. My mother never left the village, and my sister wasn't old enough to drive.

I hurried back inside and Kenna met me at the door. "You have to go after her," she said.

Immediately, I got it. "She left," I whispered. "Rowan left."

"Mother's taking her to the nearest city and buying her a ticket on a ship offworld."

"Roots and branches," I breathed, running hand over my horn.

"You can borrow a transporter from someone else," said Kenna. "Also, I'm coming with you."

I kept rubbing my horn.

"You're going after her, aren't you?" said Kenna.

My lips parted.

"Roots and branches!" She glared at me. "What's wrong with you? She's your mate. You can't let her go."

I swallowed. "No, of course I can't." I winced. "But I need another pair of pants." Because mine were ripped. I rushed away from my sister and headed for my bedroom.

Our room.

It smelled like her, even though she'd taken all of her clothes out of the closet and stripped every sign of her from the place. It shook me, actually, how little there was of hers in this place, how easy it was to erase her.

I hadn't chosen this, hadn't asked for a mate, but losing her would devastate me.

Kenna was at the door. "You're taking your time," she accused. "Don't you like her? I like her a lot."

"Of course I like her," I said, pushing past her.

She came behind me in the corridor. "You're not acting like it."

"I'm not sure that I'm exactly good for her," I said. "I think maybe she figured that out."

"Of course you're good for her, Hugo," said Kenna. "You're my big brother and you're…"

I turned to look at her.

"I mean I guess I don't really know a lot about you," she said, running one of her fingers around the shimmering pattern on one of her horns.

"You and I should spend some time together," I said. "Reconnect."

"You've been sort of preoccupied, though, because you're mated," she said. "Which is really romantic, except you're not being romantic now."

"You kidding? What's more romantic than a chase to the spaceport?" I let out a little laugh.

"Well, we're not chasing," she said. "We don't even have a transporter."

"Right," I said. "We do need a transporter."

* * *

hugo

"What is wrong with you?" Gonn was saying.

"You going to let me borrow the transporter or not?" I said. I was standing in the doorway to Gonn and Rrila's house. I knew they had one, because they went into the city once or twice every moon-cycle. I also figured that, since they knew Rowan, they'd be sympathetic to my plight.

"I hear that you yanked her out of the tavern looking like murder," said Gonn.

"No, it was mating madness," I said.

"Well, if that's happening, why aren't the two of you on a noccht?"

"It's complicated," I said.

He lifted his chin and looked me over.

"If I can get her back, I'll have to remedy that," I said. But, really, what was I going to say to her that could possibly convince her? I knew I wanted her around, but I couldn't think of one single good reason she should stay. It had always been crazy, the two of us, but she'd been up for crazy. She'd been... adventurous and a little wild and impulsive and ready for anything.

Maybe that was the reason I loved her, honestly.

Roots and branches.

Why would I accuse her of being fucked up, when it was me? It was all just *me*.

"She'd be good for the clan," said Gonn. "She was asking all about the plans for a lumber business, and about opportunities we have here to earn credits and things. A lot of the guys at the tavern practically worship the ground she walks on at this point. I mean, your mother would never set foot in that tavern, and she just walked in there and started *listening* to them."

"Did she." I blinked. "That's why she was there? What's this lumber thing?"

He shook his head at me. "You're the chieftain, and you don't know a thing about your whole clan, do you?"

My lips parted. Then I found I couldn't meet his gaze.

"So, if you were jealous or something—"

"No," I said, looking back up at him. "No, I didn't think..." Maybe I sort of was.

"I get that, during the first stages of the bond. It's hard to stay in control of yourself, which is why you two shouldn't even be here, but off by yourselves."

"Her body isn't like our women. She has this cycle-thing, and I thought I needed to be here to resume my duties." Which I had not been attending to at all, in fact.

"Well, I think you should try to get her back."

"Which is why I'm here for your transporter!"

"Oh, yeah," he said, looking a little sheepish. "Sure, it's in the garage. I'll open it up for you."

TWENTY-THREE

hugo

Once the transporter was fired up and we were speeding up over the tops of the trees, heading toward the city, I realized I should probably try sending Rowan a message on her bracelet.

That was actually probably the first thing I should have done.

Who had suggested racing after her? My overly romantic adolescent sister?

Anyway, I sent the message. *Don't go. Let's talk.*

She sent back, *It's not really about you. It's just who I am, I think. I'm stupid. We don't need to talk. This is going to be better for everyone.*

You're not stupid. Please. Let's talk.

But she didn't send anything back, not to that message or the five other ones I sent before I decided to give up.

I messaged my mother instead.

I know you're angry with me, but I really don't think she's a good fit for you or the clan, my mother replied.

Are you with her right now?

No, I dropped her at the spaceport. I'm on my way home now.

I stopped messaging my mother, also, who was worthless.

Then we got stopped by traffic controllers, because of course we did. In the city, transporters had to be carefully controlled, flying only in certain patterns and altitudes, or they'd otherwise run into each other. Transporters were equipped with sensors and auto-evasive-maneuvers, which was typically enough in a rural setting, but in the city, the transporter's navsystem needed to lock into the city's grid. It would take our destination and adjust our course to make sure we got there in the most efficient way possible.

Well, that was the theory, anyway.

In practice, there were always delays.

I sat at the navscreen, scrolling through traffic maps, trying to figure out why we were stopped.

Kenna bounced in the seat next to me, babbling constantly that if we didn't get moving we weren't going to be able to catch her.

I'd had a friend in university who had taught me a trick, one that meant I could override the traffic controllers and chart my own course, but it would mean that I'd have to take manual control of the transporter and actually steer it through the city streets, which sounded precarious.

On the other hand, what if we climbed up to the high altitude lanes, where travelers went if they were bypassing the city entirely?

Then I could just swoop over this mess and get right to the spaceport on the other side of the city.

It could work.

I switched over to another screen and typed in my friend's code.

Then I waited, heart in my throat, unsure if it was going to work. The screen flickered and then turned black and then reappeared, but now it was framed with a red line that flashed, indicating that I was flying without any benefit of the controllers and that I was also invisible to other transporters.

"What did you do?" said Kenna, leaning over.

"Buckle up, Kenna," I said, taking hold of the steering sticks.

She did, wary. "Hugo, are you going to get us killed?"

"Hope not." I pushed in the button on the left to accelerate and pointed the steering sticks upward.

The transporter roared to life, and we shot straight up, the buildings and transporters surrounding us turning to streaming lines as we revved past them.

Another transporter was coming from the left, right into our path.

I swerved.

We were tossed sideways into our seat belts.

Kenna screamed.

Oh, there was another one. It was coming straight for us, and it was bright green.

I swerved the other direction.

"Hugo, roots and *branches!*"

But now we burst through the purple, fluffy cloud cover of Abbunia and now we were in the high altitude lanes, the sun burning down on us as I swerved the transporter clumsily into a lane in between two swiftly moving transporters.

Kenna uttered a keening noise, clutching the hand rests on her seat. She was muttering roots and branches under her breath over and over.

I accelerated again, and we took off.

I had to watch the map to know when we'd be near the spaceport, and we had to be doubly careful not to get in the way of the ships that were taking off and landing, since we weren't on any of the controllers' radar or visible in any other transporters' computers.

This friend of mine from university? He was a little bit of a daredevil.

When the spaceport was directly below us, I began to slow, looking around me to make sure that nothing was right behind me when I did so.

A transporter appeared in the rearview screen, chugging toward us.

"Roots and branches!" I jammed down on the a button next to the steer sticks.

We shot down into a lower lane.

The transporter zoomed overhead, rocking us in its wake.

Kenna moaned.

"We're good, Kenna, we're good," I said. I searched the maps and then lowered us another lane and then another.

Below us, now, it was churning traffic, lines and lines of slow-moving transporters, inching along.

I was not getting into that mess again.

We just needed to park. Where was the short term parking lot?

There.

I moved the steer sticks.

"I'm going to be sick," said Kenna. "When was the last time you manually drove?"

"I don't know, ten gecycles ago," I said, as the transporter whipped around, tossing us this way and that.

But in moments, we were setting down in a parking space, and I had to log back into the system to make sure that we'd be logged as paying customers in the lot and wouldn't get towed.

That done, Kenna and I got out of the transporter and ran for the entrance to the spaceport.

I typed a message to my mother. *Where was she headed?*

I don't know, my mother sent back. *What are you doing? Are you going after her?*

Messaging my mother? Less than useful.

Okay, Rowan would go back home, right? Where else would she go?

We entered inside a set of doors and above us, on a floating holoboard, was a list of arrivals and departures. I looked for something to Kalion.

Nothing to Kalion.

Of course not.

She'd have to get a connection. So, where would she go that would be close to Kalion, but would definitely be a big enough place that it would have direct connections to that planet?

I scanned the board, unsure.

"Roots and branches," I muttered. I got out my bracelet and tried messaging her again. *I'm at the spaceport. What dock are you at?*

Nothing from her.

Please, Rowan, don't we owe it at least one last conversation?

Nothing.

"What did you do to her?" said Kenna.

Oh, I don't know, I thought. *Called her a slut. Left bruises all over her body. Said she was fucked up. Forced myself on her more times than I can count.* I shrugged at my sister. "You know, normal adult relationship stuff."

She gave me a look that said she did not believe anything out of my mouth.

My bracelet beeped.

It was Rowan. *I'm on Dock Alpha-12. It's leaving in half a hihor. You've got until then.*

I grinned. "Come on, Kenna, let's go."

TWENTY-FOUR

"Oh," I said. "You brought Kenna with you."

Hugo glanced at his sister, furrowing his brow. "Yeah… didn't think that through." He gestured for Kenna to lift her wrist. "Let me see your bracelet."

"What?" said Kenna.

"I'm going to transfer you some credits, and then you're going to go and get yourself a really sweet drink with whipped topping and sprinkles and sit right over there, out of earshot, and drink it."

Kenna scoffed. "What?" She turned to me. "You want me here, don't you, Rowan?" Well, I thought that was what she said, but she was speaking Rrolln, and my Rrolln was still not super great, though it was better. I had been practicing, when I wasn't fucking Hugo or stressing about the Roots Gala. It was funny how I'd wasted so much effort on things that didn't matter.

"I do," I said in Rrolln. "I like you a lot. But we probably want to talk about private things."

"Too bad," she said, tilting back her chin.

Hugo shrugged. "We'll just speak in Common. She barely understands it."

I switched to Common. "Okay."

Kenna scoffed again. "You guys are the worst," she

decided.

Hugo glanced at her. He shifted on his feet. "I need to apologize. I said you were fucked up, but you're not. I'm the one who's fucked up."

"No, it *is* me," I said. "Not for the reasons you think, because there is nothing remotely abnormal about what gets me going sexually, but for other reasons."

He furrowed his brow. "What do you mean?"

"I mean, that I'm clearly, like, screwed up in the head. It's probably because of my parents. My mother, she… I tell people she died, but the truth is she just ran off and left me. She got work as a singer on one of those round-the-galaxy pleasure cruises?"

"Wow, that's, um, I'm really sorry about that, and I do want to hear about that, but do you mind going back for a hidosec?"

I raised my eyebrows. "Going back to what? I never told anyone that. It's kind of a big deal."

"What do you mean about your sexual desires being normal, because the last time I checked, getting bruised and forced—"

"Oh, of course, it's this." I rolled my eyes at him. "You're obsessed."

"That's why you left," he said. "Because of what I did to you out there in the woods."

"No, that is not why," I said. "No, that's no big deal. I loved that. It was great, and we could have played whatever kind of games we wanted to play if you could have stopped guilting yourself about it. I was thinking this when I was watching your fight, actually. I was thinking about how the primitive underpinnings of mating are, you know, brutal. Like, before civilization, we were all beasts, and there was a certain aspect of violence to sex. So, if some bestial part of us responds to that, it only makes sense. And I know you don't actually want to hurt me, Hugo. You know, apart from using that kind of stuff to get me off, you're very considerate of me and you never do anything to hurt me."

He blinked, thinking this through.

"It's just play, Hugo. It's just a game. If I was really hurt or really scared, I'd tell you, and I know you'd stop."

He swallowed. "Sometimes, the mating madness means I can't stop."

"I know, but the strands work around that, so it never crosses any lines for me. If it did, we'd work through it. But none of this matters, because I'm not staying."

At this point, Kenna sighed, turned on her heel, and stalked off in the direction of the whipped-topping-drink vendors.

With her gone, Hugo stepped closer to me. "But why aren't you staying?"

"It was something else you said." I sighed. "That thing about feeling important. You were right about that. I *am* fucked up in that way."

He drew back. "I don't even know if I remember saying that."

"You said that it was why I liked the rough sex, and maybe that is part of it, too. When you're all in that mating madness thing, and I'm the only person you can even think about, having my pussy is the only thing that means anything to you at all, that's... I mean, I never felt so important." I grimaced.

"You *are* important."

"But don't you see? That's why I did all of this." I hugged myself. "I could have found some other way to pay off my debts, but I just wanted people to look at me. I just wanted to be the center of attention. And then you… the way you make me *feel*." I shook my head. "And then I was going to be a chieftess, and I would matter to a whole clan."

"You're good with the clan," he said. "You're not like that at all. You care about them, and you're trying to make things better. You're a good chieftess, and the fact you like the attention, it's probably a good thing, because we have very public lives with the clan, and I need a woman who can thrive in that situation. None of that makes you fucked-up at all."

"Yes it *does*." I said it really loud.

Other people in the spaceport turned to look at us.

I cringed. I lowered my voice.

He stepped even closer. "It really doesn't."

"Look, Hugo, what kind of woman does this? Signs herself up to get fucked in an arena in front of an audience, by a strange man whose strong enough to kill her with his bare hands? What kind of woman then decides, after knowing that man for only days and barely being able to communicate with him—after *one* conversation—to mate with him and go away with him to his planet? Does this sound like a particularly stable and rational sort of woman to you?"

He kissed me.

I shoved him off. "Don't."

"Sorry." He was grinning. "Rowan, it's just… those are all the things I love about you."

I drew back, and my heart skipped a beat. "What?" His words had reached inside me and flattened me.

"You're brave," he said. "You're wild. You're eager. You're not afraid of anything and you're willing to try. Once you commit to something, you throw yourself into it wholeheartedly, and you expect excellence from yourself. You… I keep telling you you're perfect."

My mouth opened and no sound came out.

"Come home," he whispered, curling one big hand around my jaw. "I love you."

"B-but… I'm screwed up and I need to go and… and fix myself. I can't just stay here and keep doing crazy, impulsive things!"

"Yes, you can. Please, I need you to be with me and do impulsive things and make me feel alive and fix my clan and help me accept all these rough edges of myself. Because, don't you see, it's the same for both of us. I think I'm fucked up because of how you turn me into this savage who can't stop himself from having you, and you *like* that about me. And you think you're fucked up because you're impulsive and you like attention, but I like that about *you*."

"You thought I was into voyeurism, and you didn't like that."

He tilted his head to one side. "Okay, well, every time we've done it in front of a group of people, I've really enjoyed it. Maybe I haven't been honest with myself about what turns me on, because I've got all this baggage from the arena."

"I can handle your baggage," I said. "I can handle all of that."

"I know you can," he said.

"But you have to *talk* to me about it."

"I just… I feel so ashamed of the things I feel."

"Don't be," I said. "Please don't be." I kissed him.

He engulfed me in his huge arms, pressing me into his hard chest, and I opened my mouth to him, and we kissed like a whirlwind, like we were spinning in the midst of a swirling shower of stars.

And then he jerked away from me, sucking in a deep breath.

"Mating instinct rising?" I whispered.

"I have it under control," he said. "Because it might be hot here in front of the spaceport, but not in front of my little sister."

I giggled. "Definitely not."

We both turned to see Kenna coming toward us, face lit up with a huge smile. She hugged us both, getting whipped-topping all over us. "I knew you guys would make up!" she said.

TWENTY-FIVE

I had the cool box open in the noccht cabin where Hugo and I were going to be staying for the foreseeable future. "There's so much food here. Who stocked this? How long did they think we were going to be here?"

Hugo's voice filtered out from the other room. The cabin had two rooms. A kitchen-dining combo and a bedroom, since we were basically just supposed to fuck and eat enough to stay alive until he knocked me up. "My mother thinks human reproduction sounds ridiculously complicated, and she thinks it's going to take us several of your cycles to get anywhere, so she thought we needed a lot of food."

His mother. When he'd returned with me, I thought she would have been angry, but she mostly seemed resigned. She also listened when Hugo said they should talk about the lumber company for the clan, and she'd even been kind of nice to me lately. I wouldn't say we were going to be mother-in-law and daughter-in-law besties, but maybe we wouldn't murder each other?

It wasn't perfect, but Hugo was pretty close to perfect, so…

Well, I wasn't going to complain. Much.

I shut the cool box. "I'm going to make you

something from Earth, then."

"Oh, right, you can cook. I forgot about that."

"I have many talents," I said, going through the pantries and looking for some flour. I knew exactly one Earth recipe that my mother had taught me. Her grandmother had taught it to her. It was called stroganoff, and it required making noodles, and then to sour some cream and stew some meat. It was a bit of an undertaking, honestly, but it was delicious.

"I know you do, because you never do anything halfway."

He was right. I was impulsive, but once decided, I was committed. So, this thing with Hugo, it was for real, and I wasn't going to back out of it.

"Are you going to stay out in the kitchen or are you going to come back here and let me impregnate you?"

I snorted. "We should pace ourselves, don't you think?"

He appeared in the doorway. "Okay. So, then were you serious about letting me put my cock in your ass?"

My eyes widened. "You don't just… throw that out there like that."

"I don't? I thought it was cool with us doing stuff like that now." He gave me a wicked look, one that bespoke the fact that we were now regularly incorporating dirty talk into our sex, something that he had taken to easily enough once he truly felt he had permission.

Weirdly?

Less nightmares about the arena. Maybe he needed permission to explore some of that darkness within him, I didn't know. I also knew that a little bit of deviant sex wasn't going to fix all the trauma he'd been through over the years, and I was okay with whatever he needed. We were in this for the long haul, and it might take time.

"It's not a way to impregnate you," he said, grinning, and his grin was wicked too.

"No, it's not, and we're in the make-babies cabin."

"If you want to say no, that's fine," he said. He waited.

I just eyed him. My breath was getting a little shallow.

"I notice you're not saying no."

I bit down on my bottom lip. "I think you have to work up to it."

"Which… how would I do that? By bringing it up and then wearing you down with all the talk about how you should give me your virgin ass and how much I promise to be really careful with you if you do?"

My mouth was dry.

"You said you thought the strands would make sure it didn't hurt you."

"I know." Now my voice was insubstantial. "But it's kind of a big deal."

"I know it is. Which is why I want it," he said, and he loped across the kitchen to wrap an arm around me. He nuzzled my ear. "Do we work up to it by getting you really turned on? Do I worship your nipples and your pussy and make you come on my tongue first?"

"Well," I said archly, "I mean, that doesn't sound like it would be a bad strategy on your part."

He chuckled. "All right then. Let's see what we can do about your clothes, then." He started to peel my shirt away.

I helped, and I pulled his off too. "Letting me see you without your shirt might get me more turned on," I told him.

"Well, anything for that," he said and he just stood there, gazing at me with half-lidded eyes while I explored the hard planes and angles of his chest, lingering where his fur accented his pecks and belly. His breath began to grow a little more labored, a little growl with every exhale.

Finally, he stopped me, sitting me up on the counter. "The madness triggers differently now that your implant is out, and it's slower, but it's still there. I want to take my time with you, so let's slow down for a bit."

So, then we just kissed, neither of us touching the other. My shirt was off though, and my bare breasts kept rubbing against the fur on his chest, which felt good and made them get a little stiff, and when his mouth traveled over my neck and down my chest to apply his dark, wet tongue to the slopes of my breasts and eventually my nipples, I was already tingly and a little aroused.

Well, maybe I spent all my time in a state of half-arousal with this man.

"I love the way you taste, Rowan," he murmured. "I love the way your skin is so smooth when I lick you."

I gasped and arched my back and presented my breasts to him. "Your textured tongue is nice. I like your tongue. I like that you're so interested in licking."

He just chuckled and licked me more. He licked me up and down and side to side and in circles, and he grunted that he was going to lick me until he could smell my arousal and that was when he was going to lick me between my legs.

I let him take his time.

When he did take off my pants and put his face between my thighs, he seemed to enjoy it there as much as I did, and he started lapping at me.

In between, he breathed into my pussy that this was what he'd wanted to do with me the first time he'd seen me. "I just wanted you spread out like this in front of me, for me to run my tongue all over you."

I rolled my hips against his textured licks. I groaned and urged him on.

"Are you mine, Rowan?" he said.

"Yes, I'm yours, Hugo."

"Then you do what I like, don't you? You do what I want you to do, and I want you to come for me."

"Make me come, then," I said. "If you want it, you have to get me there."

He laughed into me, redoubling his efforts.

I began to feel as if I was inside a warm, dark space, all of its warmth and darkness pressing into me. The squeeze grew tighter and more intense, all of it good and getting better with every stroke of his tongue.

"Who do you belong to?"

"I'm Hugo's."

"You're my good girl?"

"Yes," I gasped, feeling everything tighten on me, exquisite.

"Then come for me like a good girl."

I moaned, the exquisite feeling growing, taking me over.

"Come all over my mouth, just like that, Rowan. You can do it."

I gasped.

"That's it, there you go. That's good. Very good."

And I did. I came, twitching against his tongue, and then I clamped my legs together and rode out the orgasm, sighing and whispering his name.

He picked me up and carried me back to the

bedroom. He put me on the bed and climbed over me, and we kissed as he removed his pants.

His cock was just as big and pretty as it always was. I wrapped an appreciative hand around it and tickled the edges of his strands as they floated in the air.

"So?" he said in a soft voice. "Are you going to give me your ass, Rowan?"

"You are so big," I said, rubbing his cock, which was way too big to fit in my pussy, let alone my ass. How did I even take this thing? I felt a rush of adrenaline shooting through me and I was nodding. "Okay, okay, sure. You can fuck my ass, Hugo."

"Your virgin ass," he said.

"I told you that."

"You're giving me your very tight, very unfucked, very pretty asshole."

I wriggled into him. "You are way too turned on by this."

He grinned. "I know. It's probably wrong. I want so many wrong things with you, Rowan."

We kissed, tongues eager against each other.

"Just." I was panting. "You said you'd be careful, so you will, even while I'm letting you indulge and do all the wrong things with me?"

"Very, very careful," he breathed. "I swear."

"Okay." I drew in a breath, squaring my shoulders.

He caught me by the chin. "Hey, look at me."

I met his gaze.

"You would say no?" The timbre of his voice had changed, and there was only concern in it. "You wouldn't give me this if you didn't want it?"

I touched his face. "Not if I didn't want it."

"And if you change your mind, we'll make it stop."

"In the middle of the mating madness?"

"Elbow me in the throat," he said, deadly serious.

I giggled.

"Rowan, maybe we shouldn't."

"We should," I said, giving him a mischievous grin. "We really should. Come on, Hugo. Don't worry. It's okay." I flipped over, spreading out belly-down on the bed. I glanced at him over my shoulder. "I'm yours, Hugo," I said in a throaty voice. "Take my ass and make it yours, too."

He groaned.

One of his hands went between my legs to stroke my sensitive pussy, and my just-orgasmed clit gave a little clench as he rubbed it.

I gasped.

His other hand palmed one of the cheeks of my ass, and it was warm and enormous, and I felt myself shot through with excitement and apprehension and curiosity.

"Spread your legs, Rowan." His voice was like deep space.

I did.

"Wider," he said.

I did.

His thumb stroked the bud of my asshole, even as his other hand circled my clit.

It didn't feel bad, actually, it felt… well, I was sensitive there, and I made an encouraging noise, writhing a little against the bed, which caused some gratifying friction with my already-sensitive nipples, so I did it again.

"This is… have I told you how perfect you are?"

"Only several times a day," I managed.

He bent over me, kissing my neck and then the notches of my spine. He kissed his way down to my lower back, and then settled himself closer to me.

The first thing I felt was a strand, burrowing in between my pussy and my asshole. It shot an electric current straight to both my clit and my nipples and I let out an appreciative sigh.

Then there was another strand, above my opening, and then the others nestled in, and the head of his cock was pressing against me there.

I panted, tensing, because he *was* too big.

This was impossible.

Immediately, I could feel his cock was spurting out some thick, liquid, and I felt the tip of him start to work its way into me.

I tensed again, just out of instinct, and the strands shot straight into my muscles and relaxed them. They sent more pulses into my clit and my nipples, and I groaned as the head of his cock pushed its way into me.

Through the strands, I felt how good it was for him. I was so snug around his cockhead.

"Rowan," he breathed. "How are you doing?" He was kissing my shoulders, my neck.

"Good," I said. I was breathing hard.

"You sure? Am I hurting you?"

"No," I said. It didn't hurt, but it felt… different. "You can feel I'm not hurt through the strands."

"Yeah, I guess. Just… making sure. Can you take more?"

I just breathed, and I lifted my hips experimentally, taking a little more of his girth. "Yeah," I whispered. "Give me a little more of your cock."

He grunted and complied.

There was more liquid coming out of his cock, easing his entry, and the strands relaxed me even more. Even so, I was incredibly tight around him, and I could feel him with startling detail. It wasn't anything like having him in my pussy. I could feel the ridges of him. I was hugging him like a glove.

He liked it.

I liked him liking it, and I liked it too.

I moaned.

He moaned.

The strands pulsed me.

"Oh, give me all of you, now, please," I begged.

"Yeah," was all he could say as he settled himself, buried to the hilt in me.

I turned my head to find his lips.

We kissed long, deep, slow kisses, both of us moaning, and he started to move in me.

I cried out.

"Fuck, Rowan," he breathed, his hands going to my hips.

I arched my back, pressing my forehead into the bed. He felt so big and I felt so full of him, and this was… wow, this was incredibly intimate.

His mouth was at the base of my neck, and I felt his pleasure come through the strands, and it was *good*, but there was some other quality to it, something I hadn't expected. I thought this would be like… I don't know… like some kind of very kinky dominance play, and it didn't feel like that at *all*.

The strands pushed pleasure into me, and it was like rainbows, surges of bright, hot pleasure that racked me, and I felt invaded so sweetly, so claimed, so good. "I'm yours, Hugo," I whimpered. "I'm yours, I'm yours, I'm yours."

"No, no, no. I'm *yours*. You own me. You *possess* me. I worship you." He was making slow, deliberate strokes in me, and every single one made the rainbow strands that were connecting all my sensitive places go tighter and brighter and better.

I pressed back into him, wanting more of him somehow, wanting all of him, wanting full of him.

He held onto me and worked his way into me, mouth against my spine, his breath coming in harsh, affected gasps. I could feel how good I felt to him, how tight and sweet and intense, and that fed my pleasure.

The rainbow got blindingly bright, and I was awash in it, in excruciating pleasure.

I bowed up, throwing back my head, and Hugo swelled with me.

We came at the exact same moment, and the orgasm pushed into the strands and knocked me into another peak of pleasure and then bounced into him and back again, over and over, more times than I thought I could handle and then…

Finally, we were spent.

He collapsed into me, kissing anything he could get his mouth on.

I tried to turn, but he was still inside me, and the strands were still locked on, so I kissed anything I could kiss until we were finally able to get extricated enough to find each other's mouths and then we couldn't get enough of each other.

He crushed me into him, smoothing his large hands over my back.

I ran my fingers over his massive shoulders.

Our foreheads touched.

"Thank you," he whispered.

I let out a soft laugh.

"No, I mean it, I feel humbled by that, like it was… like it was really a gift."

I kissed him.

"Fuck, I love you. Sometimes, I can't even fathom how much I love you. It's so much."

"I love you too. So much too." I giggled, because it sounded stupid after what he said, which was practically poetry.

"Rowan, Rowan, Rowan." He was pushing my hair away from my face, putting kisses all over my face, and I was clinging to him.

It was good.

It was perfect.

We slept.

When we woke up, I straddled him and rode him until we both exploded again.

I tried to find time to make stroganoff, but he kept me pretty busy.

It did not take cycles and cycles for me to get pregnant.

Not at all.

TWENTY-SIX

hugo

The bond was supposed to change once she was pregnant, and it did, sort of. The madness stopped rising, though it hadn't been really intense in a while, that out-of-control explosion in my brain where I could barely talk and couldn't seem to make my limbs obey. I still didn't know why that shift had happened.

Had perhaps the mating instinct been on overdrive because of the chemical hormones in her body, which had confused me so much that it had triggered the intensity? Had it simply been a side effect of the beginning of the bond, which was possibly more violent in the beginning and then tapered off, anyway, because my body could physically not handle it sustained? It was true that usually it only took a short time for men of my people to impregnate their mates.

It hadn't taken us that long either, all things considered, I supposed.

But once she was pregnant, I sort of assumed the sex would slow down naturally, and it, uh, didn't, not exactly. My bond attuned me to her, and I was her mate, so my body was there to service whatever she wanted, and apparently what she wanted was my cock, so, well, I was not opposed to the idea, let's just say.

And her body was fascinatingly attractive in

different ways as the baby grew in her.

We did find time to pay attention to the clan. My mother softened more and more every day, and a whole lot once Rowan's pregnancy was showing. It was going to be her first grandchild, after all.

Rowan was beloved by the clan. It's really the only way I can explain it. They loved her as much as I did, and they raved for cycles to come about the first Roots Gala she organized, how immaculate she had made it. They thought everything she did was wonderful, and they loved how accessible she was. She wanted to know each member of the clan. She made it her business to memorize all their names, and she listened carefully to all of their concerns and worries.

She was the best thing that ever happened to me, but she was probably the best thing that ever happened to the clan also.

I'd be lying if I said we never argued or that it was always smooth sailing or that we had no problems. Nothing is perfect. But I thought what we had was about as close to perfect as two people could get.

It seemed to me that what we'd said at the beginning, that as long as we thought about things from the other's perspective and we kept each other's feelings in mind, we tended to be able to talk things out.

She could be crazy, and she always kept me on my toes, but that was who she was, and I wouldn't ever want her to be anything different.

When she went into labor, I was nervous.

I knew we wouldn't have been able to mate or to reproduce if it wasn't going to work, but I also didn't know of a Treebark person and a human ever having a baby together, and I worried her body was going to have trouble. Treebark people were bigger than humans on average, and she seemed so vulnerable to me.

This was something I couldn't help with, not really, and I felt out-of-control in an awful way. It was worse than being in the arena, worse than being owned, because there was no way out of it.

But we went to the city, to a Med Center there, and everyone who worked there was pretty blasé about human women having hybrid babies, because it was kind of common, so that was reassuring, and they knew all the sorts of interventions that were necessary and which weren't, and the baby was born fine.

A little girl.

She was the most beautiful thing I'd ever seen.

Sometimes, at night, when she woke up and I could tell her mother was too exhausted to think, I'd pick up our little bundle and take her out for a walk around the lagoon, and I'd whisper to her about how her mother had come from the stars, and how our little girl was part of the bigger galaxy but also part of our little clan.

She liked the movement and the deep resonance of my voice.

I liked looking into her big, expressive eyes and looking at her perfect, tiny features, including her little nubbly horns.

I don't know how to explain how good it was in those moments, in the still darkness, nothing but me and this little person in my arms, this sweet little being that Rowan had somehow given me?

It was very good.

But it was even better to come back home and crawl into bed next to her mother's sleeping form, all three of us tucked into our bed. There we would sleep beneath the tree canopy of the village, and above that, the dark purple sky of Abbunia surrounded us, and beyond that, there was space, dotted full of stars and suns and moons and planets.